THE TRUTH ABOUT
Magik AND *Dragons*

T. L. Frye

Published by DreamPunk Press
(Norfolk, Virginia)

Edited by Tara Moeller

ISBN 13: 978-1-938215-68-1 (OpenDyslexic)

www.dreampunkpress.com

AUTHOR DEDICATION

Life is messy.

If it wasn't, it wouldn't have taken me four years to get this sequel together, but that's how it went. My mother recovered from her cancer, my kid graduated high school—and college, albeit that was early. I got a new "real job" and moved—sort of.

Many thanks to everyone who helped me put this book together.

In the beginning, my kid and their middle school friends who read the first book and asked for more. In the middle, the children of my friends--Alexis, Erin, and Elizia--who read the first book, and asked for another. And for the finale, my now-grown kid, who told me to move my butt and get this done.

Many thanks to Steph C. for the awesome beta and proofread. She caught too many mistakes for my ego to tell you about.

Let's hope it doesn't take me as long to finish the next book.

The Truth about Magik and Dragons

PROLOGUE

It was night at the Summer Castle. All the servants were abed, save the guards that stood outside; even the hounds snored at the hearth. The princess crept down the hall to the library, her favorite room, silent on bare feet. Ducking into the darkened space, she paused to listen.

No one followed her.

Closing the door, she sighed and closed her eyes, leaning into the thick wood, taking in long drags of air to ease the ache in her lungs. She hadn't realized she'd been holding her breath.

Something rustled across the room.

Opening her eyes, she lit the lamps and stared up at the grand tapestry that hung on the far wall. The fabric, thick and heavy, hung from a gilded bar set at the ceiling, stretching to the floor where it pooled at the bottom. Two figures, stitched in muted colors tinted the red of the background, stood in the center, unmoving, staring out into the room.

"Good evening." Her voice rasped in the quiet. She cleared her throat, willing it not to close. Swallowing, she held the tears at bay. It would not do to let them know she cried.

The stitched man nodded and smiled; a crown rested upon his head, hinting at gold. His queen stood next to him, holding his arm, smiling down at the girl, her own tears streaking pink on her cheeks.

"I'm sorry I haven't figured out how to get you out yet." The girl stepped close, her toes brushing the bottom edge of the tapestry where it pooled on the floor.

The king waved a hand, dismissing her apology. He still smiled, and the princess knew he wasn't angry with her. He understood she couldn't do anything to help them--yet.

She reached up a hand, stroking next to the standing figures. They were life size, green-gold shadowed leaves framing their fabric portrait.

The queen lifted her own hand, meeting the flesh and blood fingers, but the princess felt no touch, no hint of warmth.

"I will get you out." Her voice stronger, louder, the princess made the vow for the hundredth, nay two hundredth time. "So help me, I will find a way."

The king smiled and nodded, reaching his own hand to where the girl's rested on the tapestry.

The three stood, as linked as they could with magic in the way, until the sun crept through the windows and the chapel bell sounded that the princess had to go back to being a princess.

CHAPTER ONE

The Princess Alexandrina Constancia Eliza of Vreden looked out over the great hall of the Summer Castle. Her people--*her people*--sat on long benches watching her. A golden coronet, adorned with rubies, emeralds, and opals, nestled in her dark curls, the loose brown ringlets now long enough to tickle her exposed shoulders. The velvet burgundy gown was new--all of her clothing was new and stiff--chosen by Gwennie and the other ladies of the court as appropriate attire for a princess to wear when meeting *her people*.

Her people. They spoke the two words like they belonged to her. But if that was the case, why did *she* have to cater to them? As ruler, shouldn't she be making the rules and having *her people* follow them?

The metal circlet was tight and heavy, pinching into the scalp. She wished she did not have to wear it, but everyone insisted that she must. People stared at it, instead of looking into her face. Sometimes, it felt like that is all they saw, and she was invisible.

Even Gwennie told her it was a necessity, that *her people* would expect her to wear it and question if she did not. So, she had acquiesced and let them place it on her head.

It squeezed her temples, making them throb. Her corset was uncomfortable, too, and the bottom edge jabbed into her right hip.

When she'd proclaimed her discomfort that morning, the court ladies in attendance had lectured her, looking down their long thin noses, their chins tipped up, eyes rolling at her audacity.

"It will stop you from slouching." Lady Mariana explained.

Ally thought she stood quite straight without the stiff boning.

"It will give you a trim waist." Lady Candace informed.

She hadn't been aware it was fat.

"If you don't wear it, your dresses won't fit." Lady Zenith warned.

They should have ordered the dresses made to fit her body.

On top of all that, the gown was too long if she did not wear the proper shoes with a heel, and too limp if she did not wear the proper underskirts with the extra poufing over her derriere.

There was more gown than there was Ally.

In her humble opinion, there were more rules than necessary to being the ruler of a country--when would she find the time to learn how to lead *her people* if she spent all her time worrying about her dress?

A low cough from her left brought her back to the present.

Baron Rothschilde, his long hair and beard a wispy white, sat to her left on the long, wide dais. One of her grandfather's favored advisors, he had been advisor to her father, King Edric, also. Now, he was advisor to her. She found that he was a wealth of information about the past, that he knew the name of all the kingdom's barons, and, even better, their allegiances.

Baron Humphrey, a younger baron, and leader of the unsuccessful revolt against King Rolando, sat to her right. It was announced that he was an advisor because of his loyalty to her father, but Baron Rothschilde had suggested she name him an advisor to make an alliance with those who had rebelled against King Rolando, an important alliance that might prevent them from rebelling against her.

Ally could not imagine why they would rebel against *her*. After all, she had been the one to finally defeat King Rolando and end his dark sorcery, freeing Vreden from his indifferent rule and preventing a civil war among the barons – so far. Some of the barons had yet to accept her as Vreden's ruler; a few were outright hostile and refused to do so.

Baron Castellan sat to the right of Baron Humphrey. He, like Baron Rothschilde, had been an advisor to her father. He had also been her father's friend, and his stories about her father's childhood had convinced her to make him her advisor and an unofficial mentor of sorts. She constantly asked him questions about what her father would have done in any given circumstance.

Except her dress. Her father, the baron had pointed out, had never, ever worn a dress. He had told her this with a smile, and that is when Ally had decided to like him.

Talk about the castle--and perhaps the kingdom--was that Baron Humphrey was aiming to become king via marriage. Ally hoped not. She could not imagine herself married to Baron

Humphrey. Even though he was young for a baron, he was still much too old for her taste. He could also be overbearing, and like to tell her how he thought she should act or decide.

As for today, the citizens of Vreden could speak to her; they could ask a question, make a comment, or offer a suggestion. So far, they had all sat on their benches and stared at her--or rather at her crown. Someone in the back coughed, and its hacking echo ricocheted about the cavernous chamber. Baron Humphrey cleared his throat. That echoed, too.

Of course, this was the first time many of them had been able to see her up close. Though she had taken to riding through the country, visiting villages and baronages, most of the people of Vreden had been working in the fields during her visits, and she had been stuck in boring conversations with the barons and their daughters and sons.

These visits had been all she had done since the beginning of summer and the ball to present and introduce her to the barons of Vreden. Many had not thought her to be the true Princess Alexandrina, but most were convinced once they saw her; she was the spitting image of her father, right down to the cleft in her chin and the dimple in her cheek.

Sitting stiff-backed in her chair, hands clasped tightly on her lap, Ally held her head up, her neck straight, and her chin out. Anything less and her corset would likely cut her in half.

The circlet continued to press into her temples.

Baron Humphrey smiled at her. Ally tried to smile back, but was unable to get her lips to curl upward.

A noise at the doors turned everyone's attention.

And Ally smiled, her lips turning up with ease and parting just a bit. Grinning, she watched the scene unfold.

Orion, prince of the neighboring Kingdom of Paixor, strode into the hall, tall and slim, smiling and nodding at those seated. He walked to the guard at the front, whispering quietly to him. The guard nodded and Orion gestured for someone else to enter the hall.

Another young man entered, his glance darting to the people on the benches, to the guards, and then to those seated on the dais. This young man was dressed in black and gray from head to toe, his clothing unadorned and simple. Even his blond hair was ashy; his pale face grey tinged and solemn.

Ally smiled at him, thinking he needed some reassurance. The young man did not smile back, but kept his eyes turned down.

Orion approached the dais and bowed deeply. The three barons rose quickly, bowing to him in turn. Ally stood last, forgetting in her happiness to see her friend, that he, too, was born royal, and should be shown deference.

Ally curtseyed slowly, not in disrespect, but to make sure that she did not topple off the dais. Standing, she curtailed a wince; her new shoes pinched her toes, a cramp spearing the instep of her right foot. She moved her foot out of the shoe, bending and flexing it to relieve the muscles.

The young man accompanying Orion moved to the front and bowed as well.

"Good morn' Princess, Barons, and good people of Vreden." Orion grinned while addressing them each in turn, nodding to them as he did. The barons sat back down; Ally remained standing. She wanted to jump off the dais and hug Orion, but she knew that it was not be the proper action.

"Good morn', Prince Orion. It is good to see you again." Ally's voice rang clear through the room, and the people on the benches shifted, craning their necks to try to see Orion's face.

"I have just returned from Paixor, the land of my birth. My father, King Mychal, sends his regards, and hopes to make an official visit soon."

Ally smiled. "He will be most welcome when he arrives." Her left foot began to cramp, and she tried to balance on her right to take some of the pressure off it. She swayed a bit, but otherwise remained standing.

It was awkward, speaking to Orion like this. They were best friends; she'd rescued him from a life of abuse as a dragon, but in front of her advisors, she needed to maintain decorum. Gwennie, and the ladies that had been chosen to train her in the ways of court, had been stressing that to her endlessly.

"May I introduce to you, Sir Oliver, also of Paixor. He has a request for you." Orion looked straight at Ally, his gaze boring into hers.

Ally thought that perhaps Orion was trying to tell her something, but she was not sure what. In dragon form, he would have been able to direct his words right into her brain.

She looked to Sir Oliver, smiling at him and nodding, trying to let him know that he could speak.

But Sir Oliver stood without speaking, a dull flush of red slowly creeping up his neck and onto his face. He shuffled his feet, looking down at them instead of at Ally.

Orion must have realized that his friend was not going to speak. "Your Highness, Sir Oliver would like your permission to pursue a quest here in Vreden." Orion watched Sir Oliver. "He is most anxious to have your blessing on this matter."

Sir Oliver still stared at his feet.

Baron Humphrey shifted in his seat. Ally did not want Baron Humphrey to make the decision about this quest, telling her what to do --especially not in front of Orion and his friend, Sir Oliver.

"Sir Oliver, please tell me about this quest." Carefully tucking her skirts, Ally sat in her chair, hoping that it would make Sir Oliver more at ease. She turned in her chair to face the young man, sneaking a quick peek at Orion, to find him watching her again, the intensity of his teal-blue gaze making her a bit uncomfortable.

Baron Humphrey leaned forward in his chair as if to speak, and Ally raised her hand to silence him.

Baron Castellan smiled into his far shoulder, his shoulders shaking in silent laughter. Baron Humphrey flushed pink, huffing back in his chair, but did not speak.

Ally watched Sir Oliver. "I cannot grant your request unless I know what your request is, good sir."

Sir Oliver cleared his throat and shuffled his feet. "Your Highness, I would like to pursue a quest for a dragon. There are many reports along the border of Vreden and Paixor that have reached King Mychal of a dragon attacking and destroying villages. I would like the opportunity to destroy this menace."

Eyes wide, Ally could not help but stare at Sir Oliver. She knew it was rude, and that Gwennie would chastise her to no end when she found out, but she could not stop herself. She closed her mouth and took a deep breath though her nose, her lungs pressing against the constricting corset. He wanted to kill a dragon? A dragon that was purportedly destroying Vreden villages?

"Sir Oliver, I have heard no such reports. Have you records of these attacks?" Ally knew her tone had become cool, but she could not help it. What if the dragon he spoke of was Orion? What if the village destruction in the stories was simply the fire Orion accidentally started when they were escaping those villagers intent on killing him and selling his scales?

Ally glanced at Orion, seeking guidance. Her instinct was to deny the request. Orion continued to stare at her, his gaze unwavering. He looked at her, and once--only once--dipped his chin down and then up.

He wanted her to grant the request? Why?

Ally pulled her gaze back to Sir Oliver, who was busy pulling sheaves of paper from a satchel strung over his back.

"Your Highness, if I may?" He held the papers out to her. Ally took them, glancing at them quickly. She noticed the fancy scrawl of cursive writing, and the elaborate signatures at the bottom of the first leaf, but she could not read them.

Sir Oliver did not know this, however, and Ally was not going to let him know. She leafed quickly through the papers then handed them to Baron Rothschilde, who took longer to study them.

"These affidavits are from Vreden and Paixor citizens who swear that they have seen the dragon. Seen it and watched it recklessly destroy villages, attacking villagers and ravaging their livestock." Sir Oliver no longer stared at his feet. He had stepped forward, the toes of his black polished boots almost touching the edge of the dais, the flush on his face no longer from embarrassment but from excitement.

Ally glanced once more to Orion, wanting to verify his desire that Sir Oliver be granted this request. Again, carefully, deliberately, Orion nodded once.

Turning her attention back to Sir Oliver, looking him up and down, Ally tried to look like she was considering his request. She hoped no one else noticed Orion's nods; she wanted everyone--especially Baron Humphreys--to think she was making this choice all on her own.

"Sir Oliver," she spoke with force, willing her voice to sound strong and sure, though it felt like the words were moving through a blockage in her throat, "you have my permission to pursue this quest, for this dragon. However," Ally felt forced to clarify her wishes when Sir Oliver looked like he would swoon from joy, "I want you to verify that this dragon is dangerous before destroying it."

Sir Oliver frowned. "But Your Highness..." He stumbled over his words, shaking his head and licking his lips. "Dragons are dangerous creatures...how can you possibly choose it over your people?"

The citizens of Vreden who were present began to murmur in their seats, shifting restlessly.

"Sir Oliver, I believe in the adage "innocent until proven guilty" and I extend that to all living creatures that reside within Vreden. For all I know, there is some reason that the beast is acting in such a manner, and that reason is the true danger to my people."

Ally stood once more, ignoring the cramp in her foot and the pinch at her hip and the ache in her temples. Too often, she and Gwennie had been assumed guilty of whatever mischief or wrongdoing had occurred, simply because they were gypsies and might have been around at the time. If she had anything to say, and as ruling Princess--soon-to-be-coronated Queen--she was quite sure she would, no one, not even a dragon or a dog, would be punished for a crime that could not be proven.

Sir Oliver backed up a pace, glancing to Orion. Swallowing hard enough that Ally could see the movement of his throat, he nodded. "Of course, Your Highness. I will do as you request."

Ally nodded, and looked at her people. They were quiet once again, staring at their new princess, some with frowns and some without, many with their mouths gaping open.

Nodding one last time, Ally gathered her skirts and swept off the dais, striding from the room, leaving the three barons to deal with any questions the gathered citizens might have.

CHAPTER TWO

Ally paced the length of her bedroom in the summer castle. It was an elaborate room that made her uncomfortable. The bed was large and ornate, with dozens of pillows and drapes. The windows, too, were heavily draped with ornate fabric, the many layers of fabric alternating in color and texture.

The floor was covered in a large, soft carpet. Ally liked the lush pile--she could remove her shoes and hose and walk around in her bare feet, feeling the softness beneath her soles, for hours. More often than not, she would take a pillow and blanket, and sleep on the floor. Gwennie didn't approve, but there wasn't much she could do other than chain her to the bed.

There was the large mirror that she sat in front of while the court ladies fussed with her hair and clothing, the large trunk that held all her fancy new clothes, the locked chest that held all her fancy new jewelry, and even the separate, private bath chamber where Ally could take a long warm bath whenever she felt like it.

It was all a bit much for the new princess. Though the surety of food and shelter was a relief, there were days when she longed for the little gypsy wagon and Murray and nothing else.

At a knock on her door, she paused midstride, turning to face the door and straighten her shoulders. "Come in."

Gwennie, her old nursemaid and protector during her childhood hidden as a gypsy, poked her head in. "Is ye alright?" She asked, opening the door fully and entering the room, then closing the door silently behind her.

Ally sighed. "I'm fine, Gwennie." She paced again, pivoting in front of the mirror to recross the room.

"Ye don' look like yer fine. Yer pacin' like a goat on a leash." Gwennie watched Ally pace, her hands clasped over her white apron, rocking back and forth, making her skirts sway.

"I'm thinking." Ally explained.

"About what?" Gwennie stopped rocking, a deep frown descending over her white brows.

"About life as a princess." Ally stopped and stared at Gwennie. "I thought life was hard when we had only a little money for food and had to run from villagers who didn't want us around." She threw her hands in the air and started pacing again. "I'm missing it, Gwennie."

"Missin' what?"

Ally stopped pacing again, her shoulders dropping. "Freedom." She whispered.

"Freedom?" Gwennie shook her head and tsked.

"I feel trapped, Gwennie. I feel like I'm in someone else's life, not mine. I don't like having to watch how I act around everyone, watch what I wear all the time, consider who I will see and what they might think. I just want to do my magic show and travel."

"Ye hated it when ye did it."

Ally nodded, slumping onto the stool in front of the mirror. "I know. I'm so confused."

"Ye've got everything ye could wish fer now. Yer a princess with a people to lead and a kingdom to rule. You just think about how proud yer father and mother will be and ye'll be right as rain."

Ally forced her gaze to meet Gwennie's in the mirror. The old woman stare bore into her, steel resolve hard in her eyes.

Sighing, she shrugged her shoulders. "I know Gwennie, it's just..."

"Yer feeling sorry fer yerself is all. So, things are a wee bit different than they were. They's a lot better, and don't ye ferget it." Gwennie marched to stand behind Ally, fussing with her curls, grabbing up a brush to fix the few strands that dared stray from the others.

"I won't, Gwennie. I know that I have a lot to be thankful for. Truly, I do." Chastised, Ally turned to look out the window, making Gwennie's brush pull at her scalp. She watched the puffy white clouds drift by on the wind. "It just gets a bit much sometimes. There's so much to remember."

"Straighten yer shoulders." Gwennie poked Ally in the back, between her shoulder blades, with the handle of the brush. "Ye need to sit straight 'n tall or no one will take ye serious-like in them meetin's."

Ally turned back to the mirror, watching Gwennie's reflection fuss over her hair and dress, poking her to make her sit this way or that.

Maybe what she really missed was the old Gwennie.

CHAPTER THREE

Dinner that evening was a tense affair. Orion and Sir Oliver sat with Ally at the head table at her request, talking mostly to each other, making plans for the quest. They were seated to her left; first Orion, then Sir Oliver.

Baron Humphrey scowled from the far left end, barely eating his favorite fried pork pie. Scowling at Ally's newest guests, he drank heavily from his goblet, refilling it several times from the pitcher of mead, which the maids kept refilling.

Baron Rothschilde sat at the opposite end of the table, watching Baron Humphrey, only sipping from his own goblet. He looked to Ally several times during the course of the meal, but said very little other than pleasantries.

Baron Castellan sat directly to Ally's right. He nudged her with his knee; even though he was her advisor, he could not show undue familiarity with the princess.

"Yes, Baron?" Ally whispered to the advisor, turning her head but keeping it tilted to listen to Orion and Sir Oliver's whispered plans.

"Today did not go well for Baron Humphrey." Baron Castellan glanced in the direction of the soon-to-be intoxicated man.

Ally glanced down the table at the baron in question. "I was unaware that he had made specific plans for today."

"I believe he intended to make a show of authority."

"Authority?" Ally swiveled to face Baron Castellan, listening fully and ignoring the hushed conversation taking place to her left.

"Baron Humphrey is ambitious." Baron Castellan spoke in a hushed tone, and took a sip from his goblet, surveying the rest of those eating in the main hall.

"So, I have heard." Ally took a gulp from her own goblet, coughing when the sweet honey receded and the bitter alcohol hit her throat.

The whispers to her left stopped and Orion leaned toward her. "You okay?" He tapped her between the shoulder blades.

"Yes, thank you. My drink chose the wrong tube." Ally set her goblet down and took a deep breath to clear her wind pipe.

Orion nodded and went back to whispering to Oliver.

Ally turned back to the baron.

"I think I would advise you, if you decide to take a trip—nay a quest—it is best you leave explicit instructions, perhaps informing myself and Baron Rothschilde of your intentions." The Baron fiddled with his goblet, sliding a sidelong gaze toward the far end of the table where Baron Humphrey's head swayed on his shoulders.

Ally stared at Baron Castellan, her mouth agape. How could he possibly know she wanted to tag along with Orion and his friend on their dragon-hunting adventure? She closed her lips, pressing them tight together, when she realized that Baron Rothschilde was staring at her.

"Just to be safe, Your Highness. I would not want you to return from a trip to find your throne taken from you." Baron

Castellan glanced at Orion and Sir Oliver. "With your approval, of course, I believe it might be best if a member of the royal court were to accompany our guests on their dragon quest."

Frowning, Ally considered the suggestion. Who could she send? She did not think Sir Oliver would like her interference. He already disliked the caveat she had placed on the quest.

Baron Castellan smiled at her. "In disguise, of course. We wouldn't want to stir Sir Oliver's temper."

In disguise? Baron Castellan was suggesting that *she* go with Orion and Sir Oliver as a gypsy? She knew she could do it; she had lived that life until a few short months ago. But should she?

Oh, but she wanted to.

Ally raised her goblet to Baron Castellan. "I will take your advice under consideration."

She finished eating her dinner in slow bites, counting to herself for each mouthful; *twenty-eight, twenty-nine, thirty, swallow, and then a sip of drink.* As soon as she permanently put her fork and dagger down, everyone else would have to stop eating. She thought it silly; after all, several folks in the hall did not even get their food until those at the head table were almost done. And it would be cold, to boot.

Though no longer hungry, she could see that a few people at the last table were still eating with gusto, so she played with the last bit of roasted pheasant on her gold-trimmed platter.

To her left, Orion and Sir Oliver stopped talking, and Sir Oliver gushed a sigh. He was finished and ready to be away, but could not until she was done. Ally thought that rule of court a bit silly, as well, and would have dismissed him if she just had a bit more nerve. But Baron Humphrey was already upset with her; she couldn't afford to make him truly angry.

Not if he was looking at taking her throne, either through marriage or other means.

Orion winked in her direction. He too was finished eating, but must have caught her checking those at the end table, for he was not impatient to leave like his friend.

Baron Castellan relaxed back in his chair, speaking quietly to Baron Rothschilde, who was leaning over the table so that he could be heard.

Baron Humphrey slouched against the table, goblet still in hand. His eyes were half-closed and his mouth had drool pooling in one corner, dripping down to wet the table. He was drunk. She knew the look from past experience, and fervently hoped he was the type of drunk who got sleepy rather than violent.

Noticing those at the end table were starting to talk instead of eat, she placed her fork and dagger on her plate, signaling she was finished. Immediately, kitchen maids came from the sides of the room, picking up trenchers and cups and goblets, and removing them to the kitchens.

Ally stood, managing to push her chair back without knocking it over, though it wobbled and she had to put a hand on the back to steady it. Baron Castellan and Baron Rothschilde stopped speaking and looked to her; Baron Humphrey snored.

"Have a good evening, sirs." She nodded at each in turn, even those eating at the other tables.

She left the hall in a rush, not caring what anyone thought, needing to think and make her own plans. She rather hoped that Baron Humphrey woke with a splitting head and a roiling stomach in the morning. Seeing her steward near her favorite room--the library--she asked him to let Baron Castellan and Baron Rothschilde know to meet her there when convenient.

They would come the instant they received her message, even though she truly meant that they could come when they were able. She knew they still had their own holdings to take care of and business to attend to.

Entering the library, she settled into the overstuffed chair behind her desk and pondered the unlit fireplace. Had Baron Castellan honestly been suggesting that she go with Orion and Sir Oliver? It seemed that was his intent. But she didn't know him well enough to be certain.

A knock signaled the arrival of at least one of the barons. She bade the knocker enter, and found both men had arrived. Baron Rothschilde entered last and closed the door behind him, bowing when he turned back to her. "You wished to see us?"

Ally considered the two men. She was still new to being a princess, and often asked for their help or opinion. She was most comfortable asking these two, and not Baron Humphrey.

"Yes. Please sit." She waved at the two chairs flanking the mantle.

The two men sat, Baron Rothschilde in the chair to her right; Baron Castellan in the chair to the left. In identical moves, the men leaned back, crossed one leg over the other, and steepled their fingers, watching her the whole time.

"Baron Castellan..." Ally found she could not quite voice the questions she wanted to ask. She fidgeted with her skirts, twisting her fingers into the soft fabric, fisting her hands to make them stop. Gwennie would not appreciate the added wrinkles.

"Yes, Princess. I think you should accompany your friend on the quest for the dragon." The baron grinned at her.

Ally started, surprised that he had guessed what she wanted to ask. She looked to Baron Rothschilde, only to find him with his feet now stretched out in front of him, his hands clasped in his lap, grinning at her as well. "And I agree, Princess."

Looking from one advisor to the other, she clamped her mouth closed and frowned at them.

"Princess," Baron Rothschilde leaned forward, dangling his hands between his sharp knees, "we both recognize that life as a royal is new for you, and that you are not making an easy adjustment. Even your father and mother would take breaks from the madness of being rulers."

Surprised at hearing this, Ally glanced to Baron Castellan, who nodded. "It is true."

"It can be rather trying having to be perfect all the time. Your mother had no trouble but your father..." the elderly man shook his head, silent laughter shaking at his shoulders. "He was often quite frustrated at the restrictions --and he was raised to become king!"

"So, I have support from both of you to accompany Orion and Sir Oliver? I will not find another on my throne when I return?"

"Not as long as you return within the month. If you take more than a month, I cannot guarantee that Baron Humphrey will not take action. I think he has concluded that he will not be marrying into the kingship." Baron Castellan smirked, shaking his head in disgust.

Ally licked her lips, then bit the bottom one, excited. An adventure. It was just what she needed to quell her dissatisfaction of the turn her life had taken.

"But, be serious about the month, Princess. There are steps that Baron Humphrey can take if you are gone longer than that. An absent ruler is not an effective ruler. And Baron Humphrey has the support of many of the barons who opposed King Rolando and were willing to stand against his oppressive rule. If he convinces them that you are also an ineffective ruler, he could convince them to stand against you."

"At the same time," Baron Castellan shifted in his chair, smoothing his jacket, "living among your people without them knowing who you truly are can be beneficial. It is one of the things that made your father so effective--he understood their hardships, how they lived and worked and played."

Ally nodded. It was time to make her own plans. She would not tell Gwennie; she would let her advisors do that. She would not tell Orion or Sir Oliver, either. Sir Oliver would never agree to her accompanying them, not that he could truly stop her. She could force it by telling him she would retract her permission for the quest.

And she thought she might enjoy surprising Orion.

CHAPTER FOUR

The small ballroom was quiet and dim. Ally took a breath and lit a lamp, then another and another, until the flickering flames chased the darkness away. Sniffing, she wiped the back of her hand across her nose and stepped forward.

She didn't need the light to find the tapestry, but she couldn't see it in the dark, see the figures stitched in within. It hung, centered between two great windows, right where she'd asked. The library had been nice, but too quiet for her parents, she thought. But folks passed through this room every day, smiling and bowing at the King and Queen, once again showing them the respect they deserved.

The drapes were drawn shut, and Ally had yet to find the ropes to maneuver them open. Whenever she asked, the maid would pretend she hadn't spoken. Too many around here thought Princesses shouldn't open drapes, or move their chairs or cut their meat on their platters.

"Hey." She wasn't sure they could hear her, and she only ever whispered, lest someone discover her speaking to the wall hanging. She didn't think some would understand or even believe.

The man, tall and dark-haired, smiled and dipped his head. He could not speak back, but he always responded to her words with an action.

A slight woman crossed the surface to stand at his side, reaching out for his hand. He kissed the woman's temple and pulled her close.

Careful, Ally ran a finger along the cheek of the woman's face. Her mother. It was hard to grasp that these people--trapped--were her parents.

"I won't be able to visit for a little while. I'm going on a hunt."

The woman straightened from the man, frowning, shaking her head so that the small crown on her head wobbled.

Ally smiled. "Not that kind of hunt. Not with the dogs. But a more intellectual hunt, I think. For a dragon."

This time it was the king that frowned and gestured with his hands, making a fist with one, and flapping the other near is bent elbow.

Laughing, Ally shook her head. "I know I already have Orion--and he's back by the way--and that is who I am going on this hunt with."

The pair in the tapestry grinned, her father elbowing her mother and waggling his brows.

Ally sighed, hard enough it made the tendrils of hair around her face pouf. "It isn't like that." But she knew the blush in her heated cheeks belied her denial. "A friend of his from Paixor thinks there is a dragon marauding along the border. We are going looking for this dragon."

Her father nodded and her mother frowned and crossed her arms.

"There is nothing to worry about. I'm going along to make sure that the dragon is treated fairly and, I guess, to get away from the castle for a bit." Ally looked down, working the toe of the slipper into the floor. "It's hard being a princess. I'm afraid I don't much like it."

The tapestry rippled, making Ally look up. Her father had stepped forward, though he was no closer to her, he was larger, and one hand was placed against his side of the tapestry.

Ally raised her own hand and placed it against his. She could only feel the weave of the cloth, the stitches from the embroidery and crewel work. She wished it were warmer, so it felt more like a real touch, but knew it to be impossible. The queen shifted, making the tapestry wave, and placed her hand next to the king's.

"And when I get back, I will work to get you out. I promise."

CHAPTER FIVE

The following morning, it was not Ally, but Alex who awoke in the royal bedchamber, tired from her late-night visit to the tapestry, curled on the floor with her blanket and pillow. Ally was shut up in the wardrobe cupboard with the satin and velvet dresses and the painful high heels and corset.

Alex rose, stretching and grinning, feeling lighter than she had in months. Grabbing up the items she'd placed out for the morning, she pulled on a linen tunic and pantaloons, followed by the simplest dress she owned --a thin lace-trimmed linen dress that didn't need a corset, and sturdy brown traveling boots, pulling her rough brown trousers on under the skirt of the dress. She rolled a second tunic and pair of trousers in a tight roll, packing it on top of the other necessities she had packed last evening in a single satchel.

Tying her hair back in a single queue, Alex smiled at her reflection in the mirror. Without makeup or jeweled circlet, it was a familiar face smiling back – a face she had not seen in far too long.

She knew that Orion and Sir Oliver would be leaving early. The servants had been busy preparing their supplies ever since she had given permission for the quest. Their horses had been made ready and supplies packed so that they could be carried by the two horses without the need of a pack horse.

Her own horse, a white mare given to her by Baron Humphrey, would also be ready and waiting. Baron Castellan had told the stable boy that the princess would be going for a morning ride with him, and that her horse would need to be ready at first light.

Though she did not like Baron Humphrey as a person, she loved the mare. She now recognized it as an effort to buy her favor, but that was Baron Humphrey's tact, not the horse's.

Smiling, Alex tucked a short bit of hair behind her ear. She did not need to take much; she was used to living day to day. She was ready.

She wished her writing lessons had progressed to the point that she could leave a short note for Gwennie, but even if Alex could have written the words, Gwennie would not have been able to read them. Baron Rothschilde would be waiting to explain everything to the nursemaid, and to give her the cover story they had concocted yesterday.

The Princess Alexandrina Constancia Eliza was going on a trip to visit her mother's family to the north of Vreden, returning from the journey in a month's time. According to Baron Castellan, this was a well-used alibi of her parents.

Her grandparents, if word got to them, would understand and know what to do and say. Baron Castellan sent a messenger late last evening to inform them of the princess' plan. They had been some of the first to visit her at the castle, and she would visit them for real very soon.

The castle was quiet, the halls still lit by candles, the hanging oil lamps still unlit, the sun not yet coming through the high slatted windows. The odd chamber maid bustled quickly by, ignoring her. Alex knew they did not recognize her outside of the fancy gowns and circlet. To them, she looked like a female servant, sent to the carefully guarded suite of rooms assigned to the princess and her ladies. If they had known the scruffy girl walking the halls, they'd have shrieked, dropped their loads, and fallen to their knees in shock.

Once she was down the first flight of stairs, and outside the female-only sanctum of the royal suite, Alex relaxed. The maids allowed to service her suite were those most likely to recognize her, even without the fancy gowns.

The next floor down housed the guest suites. Alex couldn't help but slow down and listen. Orion and Sir Oliver were sure to be up and about by now.

"Will you hurry up?" Sir Oliver's voice carried down the wide hall.

"What is your hurry, Oliver? I'm sure the dragon won't be going anywhere." Orion exaggerated his slow gait, clomping his tall riding boots on the polished wood floors.

"Gah. You're worse now than when we were children. You never took anything I wanted to do seriously." Sir Oliver stomped away from his friend.

Alex backed into the drapes of a tall window, hiding behind the thick damask.

"That's not true Oliver, and you know it." Orion skipped to catch up to his friend. "If I didn't take you seriously, would I have asked the Princess to approve your quest?"

Olive stopped and rounded on Orion. "I don't know. You did try to talk me out of it at first."

Orion nodded and bit his lip. "That is true. But only because I... I wanted to make sure you knew what you were about. That is when you produced your papers, after all."

"Can we just get going?" Sir Oliver stalked down the hall to the grand staircase.

"Breakfast first, yes? I'd like a proper cooked meal before we hit the trail. Might be my last for a while." Orion trotted after Sir Oliver. "I do remember your cooking from our camping trips with Father's steward."

Alex snickered from her hiding place, and Orion stopped, letting his friend get ahead of him and to the stairs. He glared at the blue drapes.

Sucking in her breath, Alex held it in, trying to stop the laughter building in her gut.

"Is someone there?" Orion stepped toward the curtain.

Sighing, Alex peeked around the fabric. "'tis only me."

"Only you? What are you doing?"

Alex stepped out from her hidey-hole and put her hands on her hips. "I can do whatever I like here, Orion. It is my castle after all."

Orion frowned and looked at the plain dress she wore, the simple queue. "You aren't dressed like it is. What are you up to?" He leaned forward, hissing at her.

"Orion?" Sir Oliver called from the stairs. "I thought you were hungry?"

"Coming." Orion returned the call. He turned back to Alex. "Don't do anything untoward. Remember, you're a princess now."

Alex just smiled and watched him jog to meet Sir Oliver and continue down for their meal. She followed at a safe distance, listening to the friends tease each other on their way to the great hall and what would likely be their last kitchen-cooked breakfast for the duration of their quest.

Finding a dark corner, Alex shrugged out of her dress, bundling it to shove into her satchel. She pulled out a belt and settled it around her waist, though not snug enough to suggest feminine curves. She needed to look like a boy, or her plan would never work.

The kitchens, as opposed to the near-deserted upper levels of the castle, were chaos. Pots were already on the spitting fires, the contents steaming and bubbling. Fresh baked bread, muffins, and biscuits cooled on racks on the side work surface. Uncooked pies and pastries littered the center work top, waiting their turn in the ovens.

The cook, a stout woman with several chins, shouted orders at the kitchen maids and the errand boys, all of whom bustled about, dodging elbows and pots and wet spills. Watching the cook – whose cooking she adored --Alex thought it funny the way her chins quivered when she was upset. They quivered now, though Alex could see no reason for upset.

Someone bumped past her, nudging her into the stone wall.

"'scuse me." Gwennie set a large basket of vegetables on the counter. "Here ye are, Maisie. This be the last of the parsnips and carrots in the south garden, though I think there's still some in the northern one. Oh, and the spinach is starting to come up. Little thin right now, but they may just need a bit more water."

"Thankee, Gwennie. His baroness is being a right devil this morning. Barking at everyone. 'e's got five of the maids cleaning his room already. Five!"

Gwennie sorted vegetable into piles. Alex could smell the fresh damp earth mixed with the sweetness of the carrots and parsnips.

"'e was probably sick all over after his bout of drinking at supper. Disgraceful display, that."

"Oh, aye. I 'eard all about his pouting from the serving girls." The cook grabbed up a bunch of the parsnips and dunked them under the water in the sink, swishing them around to clean off the dirt. "Then this morning, 'e 'as the gall to come in here, barking about how it weren't a proper meal fit fer the princess' guests."

One of the girls tending the fire snorted. "I'm sure if there were problems, her highness would 'ave said so."

"And been much nicer about it, too." The parsnips were dumped on a wooden counter and the cook examined her chopping blade before setting to work on the thin tubers. "That one knows how to treat her people, she does."

"I've 'eard that Baron Humphrey fancies himself her 'usband." The girl at the fire turned from her pot and directed the question at Gwennie.

Stomping feet heralded the arrival of someone wearing boots, and Alex ducked into an alcove.

"Is my breakfast anywhere near to being ready?" Baron Humphrey loomed in the door, his nose red, his cheeks pale and sweaty. "A man could starve around here before getting any decent service."

The girl at the fire spun back to the pot, stirring its contents frantically.

"It'll be done in a moment. Can't expect us to serve it to ye raw."

"I expect it to be cooked and served promptly when ordered."

Maisie stabbed the wood surface with the tip of her knife, the blade and handle waving with the fury used. "And I expect to be given the time necessary to cook it. Git out of me kitchen afore I have someone show ye out."

"How dare you speak to me in such a manner! I can have you dismissed!"

The old woman snorted and picked up the parsnip pieces, dropping them into a nearby pot. "Ye can try, what, but I'm certain her highness will have me back in an instant. Last I 'eard, she's still in charge around 'ere."

Baron Humphrey raised his chin. He looked like he wanted to spit more words at the cook, but instead he sneered and pivoted, slamming the far door behind him.

"Pompous prick." The girl at the fire grabbed a bowl from the cupboard and ladled some of the contents of the pot into it. "'is porridge is done. 'e wants sugar, what?"

"Aye. And lots of it." Maisie leaned over the bowl, her mouth puckering at the contents. "Stick a little butter and cinnamon in there, too. Is the ham slice nice and hot?"

"Aye, mum. It is." A young boy stood over a grate at another fire, sticking a slab of meat with a fork. He stabbed the fork in, picking it up so that the juices ran into the flames, spitting and crackling when they hit the hot embers.

Gwennie grabbed a trencher and the boy lay the meat on top, then the girl put the bowl of porridge next to it. "I'll take it out to him. He h'ain't cursed me yet."

Baron Humphrey's may not have been a mean drunk last night, but he surely was a mean after-drunk in the morning. Grabbing a cooling biscuit and an apple on the sly, Alex scurried out the side door before anyone could snag her and give her work to do--or yell at her for taking the food.

She paused at the door leading to the courtyard. What would Baron Humphrey do while she was away? Would he get even more mean? Would he fire Maisie and her favorite cook, and the two be long gone before she returned and could hire them back?

Slipping out the door, leaving her doubts behind, Alex easily made it to the front courtyard without being stopped. Everyone was too busy getting ready for the work of the day to pay much attention to a young boy making his way outside, presumable to start his own workday.

The horses were waiting; her own white mare standing docile next to Orion's and Sir Oliver's larger mounts. Three stable hands yawned and scratched at their heads, not quite awake yet, and likely planning to sneak off for a nap once the horses were claimed by their riders.

Approaching the one holding her mare, Alex tapped the lad on the shoulder and took the reins. The mare, recognizing the scent of her mistress, whinneyed softly. "I'll be takin' this one." Alex imitated Gwennie's manner, finding it easy to slip back into gypsy mode. "Baron Castellan needs ye te git 'is own horse ready."

The boy immediately handed over the reins to the mare and raced off to the stable, leaving the other two grimacing at his back.

As soon as the door slammed closed behind him, Orion and Sir Oliver exited the side door to the kitchens, each still eating a muffin, likely filched from the cook's baking rack.

Spinning around, Alex kept her back to them, crooning softly to her mare.

They approached, greeting the boys and their horses jovially. The boys left, running for the stable and their stolen naps.

Sir Oliver mounted first, checking his bags from astride his horse.

Orion checked his bags from the ground, sliding glances at Alex as he did. Alex held in her giggle, but it would have ruined the surprise and possibly given away her true identity. She did not want Sir Oliver discerning who she really was this early in the game.

But Orion was too observant. "Alex?"

Alex turned, holding her mare behind her. "Good morning, Orion. Hope you don't mind, but I'll be tagging along."

Orion stood like a statue next to his horse.

Sir Oliver frowned from atop his. "No you won't."

"Yes, I will." Alex stared back at the young man. It seemed he had nerve after all.

Orion said nothing, but continued to stare at her.

Sir Oliver puffed out his chest and exhaled with gusto. "I don't know who you think you are, but I make the decisions about this quest, and you are not coming. We have only enough provisions for two."

Alex looked up at Sir Oliver, smiling. "Trust me, you have enough provisions for three."

Orion sighed.

Sir Oliver made to puff again, but Orion cut him off with a raised hand.

"Alex is coming, Oliver. We have no choice. I think one of the barons is making him come with us."

"You would be correct, Prince Orion." Baron Castellan exited the castle just as the stable hand brought out his horse. "Thank you, Hugo. Run along now."

Once the boy was again out of sight in the stable, Baron Castellan continued his explanation. "It was decided that a representative of Vreden should accompany you on this quest. If you do not allow this, permission for the quest will be revoked."

Sir Oliver scowled, his face deepening to red. "This is ridiculous!"

Baron Castellan raised a steely gaze to Sir Oliver. "You are calling Princess Alexandrina ridiculous? After she has granted your request? It was not her suggestion that added a representative to your party; it was mine."

Orion regarded Baron Castellan, one brow raised to his auburn hairline. "I see. Any reason for this... *particular* ... representative?"

The baron smiled. "I am sure you will figure it out soon enough." He pulled on his gloves and looked to the sky. "I wish you happy hunting and a safe journey. I must be off on my morning ride. Baron Rothschilde will be needing my assistance soon, and I do want to be ready when he does."

He paused before mounting his steed, staring directly at Alex. "One month." He wagged his finger at her. "No more."

Alex nodded but said nothing, mounting her horse and adjusting the saddle.

Baron Castellan rode away at a gallop, in a hurry to complete his ride and return.

Sir Oliver glared at Alex.

"'tis not so bad, Oliver." Orion mounted his own horse. "I know Alex, and I know that he will be an asset on the journey."

"An asset? He is nothing but a scrawny waif!" Sir Oliver waved one arm in Alex's direction. "Look at him! What good will he be facing a dragon?"

Orion laughed and spurred his mount forward. "Oliver, you have no idea!"

CHAPTER SIX

Alex was enjoying being Alex, and not Ally, and certainly not *Her Royal Highness*, the Princess Alexandrina. Not even Sir Oliver's foul mood--which seemed to be his regular demeanor--could ruin her joy at being free again.

She was content. She was out and about--for another three weeks, anyway.

Though, it wasn't all fun. After a week, traveling south along the Vreden-Paixor border, Alex thought she might go mad. They were all getting tired, and the spats regarding authority between Orion and Oliver were more frequent. Oliver still didn't acknowledge Alex, and she was okay with that most of the time. It meant he wasn't yelling or cursing at her.

But when she saw something of interest, that might be a clue, and pointed it out, and he ignored her, making Orion point it out to him instead, she wanted to hex him. It got to the point that when he did so, she could feel the cold start to creep up her spine, into her fingers and toes, and she had to stop and put physical distance between them before her magic burst out.

She was going to lose control soon, if she weren't careful. She'd thought of returning to the summer castle, and leaving the boys to their search, but that would be letting the spoiled young man win --and she couldn't bear that. And she liked spending time with Orion. When he talked with her, Oliver ignored the both of them, and they might as well have been alone.

Except for the conversations they avoided; her magic and his dragon.

The horses were plodding in single file, following a faint path through waist-high grass.

Stopping, Oliver sat on his mount, pouting. "Well, so far no dragon; not even a footprint or dropped scale to show as evidence." His shoulder-length blond hair ruffled in the slight, cool breeze. He'd lost his last black ribbon used to tie it back three days ago. His horse pranced in place, anxious to start moving again. The young man kept a tight hold of his reins, his knees tightening to help hold the black horse still.

Alex let the mare stop alongside Orion's stallion. They both looked ahead at Oliver, but it was Orion who spoke. "What did you expect? That you would just stumble across it right away?"

Oliver shrugged. "I didn't think it would take this long, no. Not that we'd have found the dragon, but at least solid evidence." The three had been following a rough map he'd drawn that traced a path from village to village that had mentioned dragon sightings. "From the stories going around and the affidavits I obtained, the dragon was widely seen by everyone. You'd think some of them didn't even know what a dragon was!"

Alex had doubts about the evidence back when Sir Oliver had made his request, and even more so now, while they rode around the country, looking for something that didn't seem to exist. Perhaps that was Orion's plan--to ride around and not find anything, so Sir Oliver would decide to give up the search.

In Alex's opinion, the stories about the dragon, and the number of sightings, had been greatly exaggerated. She didn't offer that opinion, not even to Orion. Oliver still hadn't accepted that she was along for the adventure. She didn't want to pique his temper again, or have Orion do so on her behalf.

No, Oliver still thought she was just a peasant gypsy, someone tagging along to report back to Baron Castellan. He had even hinted that he thought that Alex was avoiding the law for some horribly demeaning transgression.

When Orion had pointed out that Baron Castellan had made the request, and that Alex hadn't just shown up out of nowhere, Sir Oliver had only snorted and rode off.

There had been no more discussion about Alex since, Orion refusing to respond to Oliver's snide remarks or questions, and Alex doing her best to ignore them.

Alex still felt more at home disguised as a boy than she did in the dresses and tiaras she had been forced to wear as Princess Alexandrina. Not even Oliver's suspicions could ruin that for her.

Orion sighed, his horse prancing a bit more energetically now that it was being held still. "Oliver," he paused, "why do you want to find this dragon?"

Oliver's haughty nose flared. "Dragons are evil creatures, and any that attack villages should be destroyed."

This was the reason Oliver always gave, and Alex wondered why Orion kept asking. She knew he had a vested interest in getting Sir Oliver to change his mind about dragons being "evil creatures," but the question was getting old.

Alex knew Orion's secret --he had a dragon inside him, and sometimes, it just had to come out. He'd been full dragon for many years, to the point of forgetting he was anything but, and Alex still swelled with the guilt of accidentally messing up the potion that might have returned him to full human. Instead, it had made him both, half and half, and neither

Oliver seemed as frustrated with the frequency of the question as Alex. "Why do you keep asking me that?"

Shrugging, Orion gazed at everything but his friend. "It just seems like you're keeping something from us."

Looking uncomfortable for the barest moment, Oliver laughed. The laugh brought Orion's gaze from the path ahead to his face. "It is you, Orion that is keeping something from me. You, too, seem highly interested in finding this dragon. Why is that?"

Alex watched Orion's face. The only emotion he showed was in his eyes. She knew to watch them for clues to his emotions--the fear, the anxiety, and the defiance--and so she saw them. She glanced to Sir Oliver, seeing his gaze fixed on the mountains to the east; the young man had missed it all.

"I do not think all dragons are evil." Orion eased the tightness of his reins and his horse moved forward. "I wonder why you do."

Oliver directed his own horse to follow Orion's. "It is common knowledge in Paixor."

Orion huffed. "That is not entirely accurate. That is a tale spread because of what happened to me. It was not a dragon that took me but the strategies of an evil sorcerer! I explained that to you when I returned to Paixor."

Alex followed slowly, allowing her horse to fall back a bit, not wanting to ride too close to Oliver.

"That does not mean that dragons are not evil." Oliver was determined to support his belief.

"That does not mean that they are." Orion was equally determined to change it.

"They are foul. They are smelly. They will kill a man."

"Many beasts are foul and smelly. That does not make them evil." Orion stopped speaking, taking care to guide his mount over a bit of rocky ground. "And many beasts that are considered good can easily kill a man."

Oliver did not respond immediately; he guided his horse over the rocks before speaking. "Name one."

Orion glanced behind. "Your horse; it could easily throw you to the ground and you could be killed."

"That would not be on purpose."

"How would you know? For a horse, that might be the easiest way to kill a cruel rider. Skillful, too, if you ask me, as no one would suspect that it had been done on purpose."

Alex didn't bother slowing down for the rocks. Her horse cantered up to them and jumped elegantly, landing easily on the other side of the obstruction.

Orion glanced up at her, grinning a bit, before looking again to Oliver. "Think about that a bit, eh?"

Oliver became quiet, seemingly to mull over what Orion had said. Alex thought it was more to discontinue the conversation.

Pulling to the side, Orion letting Oliver take the lead, and positioned himself to ride beside Alex once more. Looking at her, he raised one brow.

Alex shrugged, watching Oliver ahead of them. "He seems stuck in his ways." She spoke softly, not wanting the other young man to hear them. Though Orion's friend never responded to anything they said to each other, he wasn't deaf.

"Aye." Orion spoke just as softly back to her.

"What do you think of his dragon tales?"

Orion scrunched his nose, still speaking in a hushed whisper. "I am not sure what to make of them. Oliver has written accounts from those who saw this dragon. I cannot imagine anyone putting nonsense to paper and signing their name to it."

Alex sighed. "I suppose it depends on how much coin was attached to the signature."

Orion swung his gaze to her, even turning in his saddle. "What do you mean?"

Laughing, Alex smirked. "I am still as good as a gypsy, Orion. I know all about what a little coin can get you."

Her friend stared ahead, once again watching the back of their companion. "I am afraid that Oliver will be disappointed when we find no dragon for him to battle and destroy."

Alex watched Oliver, as well. "Why do you care? Do you want him to find this dragon? He intends to slay it--no questions asked."

Orion sighed. It was long and rushed, and Oliver glanced back at them at the sound, whipping his head back round once he realized what he'd done. "He is my friend. I remember him as a child, as my only playmate in a very isolated childhood. I want him to find what he needs. That is why I ask him "why." I would like to find another method of getting him what he needs."

Alex frowned. Oliver was once again looking ahead. She leaned toward Orion, lowering her voice even more. "What is it that you think he needs?"

"Glory."

Alex glanced ahead. "Glory?"

Orion nodded. "I remember us as young boys. I am a prince of Paixor, albeit the youngest. I was fawned over and recognized, even when I had done nothing of significance. Oliver could do something amazing, and be passed over simply because he was only the son of the castle steward. The only reason he was tutored with me was because of his nearness to me in age and his father's position, and the fact that he was being trained to follow in his footsteps. It also gave me a classmate, someone to learn with, to spar against. My brothers were all older and had already left the schoolroom."

Alex frowned. So, Orion thought Oliver needed glory?

"Do you need glory?" Alex glanced at Orion when she asked the question. He seemed surprised that she would ask.

"I don't think so. But then, I'm a prince, and everyone fawns over me, remember?" He grinned at her and then crossed his eyes and stuck out his tongue.

Alex scrunched her nose. "You like being fawned over?" She hated it, which was a big reason she had snuck away to go on this adventure with Orion. There were other reasons, but she didn't want to think about those right now.

Orion shook his head. "No, I don't like being fawned over. But I have had the experience, and I know that I don't like it. Oliver has never been fawned over, so he doesn't know if he likes it or not. He imagines he will like it though."

Alex pondered a moment. "I suppose, if you are recognized for something you truly did, it might not be so bad."

Orion snorted. "You mean, like finishing off King Rolando?"

Alex snorted back.

Orion laughed, and sped his horse to a trot to catch Oliver.

Alex just shook her head, watching the two friends talk softly ahead of her. She found herself comparing the two. Oliver's blond hair sparkled gold in the sun, while Orion's auburn hair seemed to catch fire. Orion was slightly taller than Oliver, but Oliver was broader in the shoulder and chest. Alex supposed it was because of all the sword training. Orion was lean muscle from years of living life as a starving dragon.

And there lay the biggest difference between the two friends. One was a dragon; the other a would-be dragon-slayer.

Alex sighed. She worried about what Oliver would do when he discovered that Orion had a dragon inside of him, a dragon that had to come out to play, to hunt, and to fly every once in a while. Would he change his mind about all dragons being evil, or would he, instead, decide that Orion was evil?

CHAPTER SEVEN

They followed a stream that meandered down through the valley, growing larger, other streams joining into it, eventually becoming a river. The banks on either side were a lush green; the forest on the far side, away from the three on horseback, looked impenetrable. The water cascaded over rocks, rushing and white, gathering speed. Its descent downward became steeper and the horses slowed, picking their way carefully along the path.

Alex still rode behind the two young men, watching them. They were silent, riding side by side. Her stomach rumbled, and Alex pulled a bit of dried meat from the small satchel she wore over her shoulder, and bit into it, chewing and sucking to let the meat soak up the moisture from her mouth before swallowing.

Orion heard her, and smiled back, half twisted in his saddle. "Should we stop for a bit?"

Alex shrugged and shook her head, still chewing a bit of the meat.

Oliver glanced back, a shot of annoyance flitting across his features. "We will get nowhere if we have to keep stopping."

Orion looked hard at his friend.

Swallowing, Alex raised her voice so that she could be heard. "I do not need to stop."

Oliver glared at her then shifted his gaze to Orion. "I still do not understand why you insisted we let the boy come. I am sure we could have told that baron no. I don't believe he really had the authority of Princess Alexandrina behind him."

He'd acknowledged her. Maybe he'd speak to her before they were done.

Orion did not answer his friend, but spurred his horse to a faster pace and took the lead.

Water rushed past, churning and foaming, jumping and spitting over rocks. Alex watched, imagining it in a race with the three of them. Would the water find the dragon first? Would it find a damsel? Alex frowned. Why was it always a damsel that was imprisoned by a dragon? So that it might be a knight who saved her?

Alex thought the pattern in the stories held some explanation. Gwennie had taught her to look for the pattern when telling fortunes--get the stories first, then provide a tale that matched the pattern. It was a trick, yes. There was no real magic in most gypsy fortunetelling, unless you asked Old Bertram.

Magic...

Alex thought about magic for a moment. She had not really thought about magic since the defeat of King Rolando in the castle's dungeon, except to keep it at bay. She'd been too busy discovering her new life. Too afraid that letting her magic out would cause problems.

Magic could be powerful, but it was also dangerous. If not the magic itself, then the reaction of others when they learned of it. And not to forget, the wielder of the magic could make the magic dangerous--that is what had happened with the sorcerer-king Rolando. The magic had gone to his head, and he had become an evil ruler, not just an ambitious one.

She wondered about her magic, and how she hadn't used it in so long. She had been too busy learning to curtsey and wear a dress and speak to barons to even think about using her magic. She had not been to the meadow, either. Meredith was sure to be upset when she eventually returned. Alex was certain a long lecture about her training being behind schedule or forgotten was in her future.

Having magic was innocuous enough--until someone found out. She had not told the barons about her magic; nor had Gwennie or Old Bertram. It was too risky. What if they feared her magic, like Old Bertram had at first?

It was the same for Orion. Having a dragon inside of him was innocuous enough, until someone like Oliver, who hated dragons on principle, found out and fear led them to destruction. Or greed. Dragon scales were purported to be have healing powers when ground into a fine powder. And to grind them, they needed to be free of the dragon.

Shuddering, Alex remembered almost losing Orion to a village that wanted his scales. She'd been drugged to sleep, and they almost hadn't made it out alive.

And led Orion to an unthinkable action in defense.

No one in the castle knew about the dragon inside Orion, save for Gwennie and Old Bertram. And Alex. The king and queen knew, of course, but as they were still trapped in the tapestry, they could hardly tell anyone. Not that they would if they could. Alex was sure of that.

Alex closed her eyes briefly. They had been riding all day, and though she said she did not need to stop, she was getting weary.

Alex didn't recognize the meadow at first. Snow, thick and wet and cold, crushed the once waving grass, now sodden and brown in the bottom of her footprints. Snowflakes drifted down from the leaden sky, melting on her hair and clothes. She was surprised to find that she was wearing a heavy wool cloak and fur-lined leather boots and hat. She looked for the camp.

It was where it always was, the snow cleared away from the tent and a fire burning in the open, stone-ringed hearth, a bright stabbing color against the endless white.

Alex stomped toward the camp, pushing her boots into the top crust of snow, looking about for Meredith. She could not see the woman anywhere close by. Perhaps she was in the tent, keeping warm?

A small iron pot hung above the fire, steam trailing skyward. Two stools once again flanked the open hearth, set a bit closer now, away from the cold, toward the heat.

She chose one and sat down, leaning over to examine the contents of the pot. It looked like clear liquid--water?--boiling away to steam.

"You are correct. It is just water." Meredith spoke from behind Alex.

Alex started and fell off the stool, glaring up at the older woman. She had not realized that she had voiced her thoughts. "That was not nice."

"It is also not nice that you have not visited me for many months." Meredith stood over Alex, looking down at her, her eyes dark in the shadow of her face.

"I told you before. I do not know how to come here on purpose. It is happenstance only." Alex slipped in the snow, trying to regain her seat.

"Hmph." Meredith's brushed past Alex to the other stool, her thin purple cloak swirling angrily around her.

Alex took a deep, steadying breath. "What is the water for? Are you cooking?"

Meredith snorted. "I have told you--I do not need to eat here."

Alex raised one brow. "It seems neither of us listen very well."

Instead of replying, Meredith pulled a small leather sack from beneath her cloak. "Take this and tell me what is inside."

Accepting the sack, Alex opened it and peered inside. It contained dried leaves and flower petals, made brown and yellow by time. She pulled some out, careful not to crush them in her fingers. She sniffed, slowly, closing her eyes, trying to separate the different smells.

"I can smell sage, and rose, and..." Alex sniffed again, "I think it is a type of wildflower. Devil's paintbrush? Maybe some lemongrass?"

Meredith smiled. "Very good, very good. You must remember these plants you name, though that is not what they are. Since that is what you smell, when you return, those are what you must gather to make your own floromance. Each person's magic uses something different."

Alex frowned and crumpled the pieces of brown between her fingers, the aroma intensifying. "But what is it for?"

"It is to help you see the future."

Meredith stood and moved to the small pot, removing it from the fire. She set it on the ground in front of Alex, snow spitting against its hot metal bottom. Taking a pinch of the dried plant matter, Meredith sprinkled it over the still bubbling water.

"Lean forward." She commanded, her hand gripping at the back of Alex's head, pushing it down. "Breathe in the steam and close your eyes."

Alex leaned forward, placing her face directly above the steam coming from the pot. She breathed deep, feeling the warm steam fill her cool lungs, smelling the sage and rose, the devil's paintbrush and the lemongrass. The smell of the lemongrass deepened so that it filled her, she could smell nothing but the lemongrass; she could even taste it in her mouth.

A scene appeared behind her eyelids. Orion and Oliver were jumping and running by the rushing river, yelling at something in the water, following it on shore. Alex tried to see what it was. Orion stepped into the foam at the edge, the current catching at him, trying to unbalance him. Oliver caught at his hand, steadying him, tethering Orion to land while Orion reached out, out, into the swirling, rushing water...

Alex couldn't breathe. The steam was too warm, too much. It felt like water had filled her lungs. Crying out, she opened her eyes, pressing back against Meredith's hand, breaking its grip, gasping for breath.

Meredith's face was only inches from her own. Alex could see the elder lines at the edges of her eyes, the rim of black at the edge of her green iris, and a faint scar that ran from her left temple down to her ear.

Rearing back, Alex fell once again from her stool, upending it this time and losing her hat to the snow. She scrambled back, gasping, drawing in the cold air, the scent and taste of lemongrass fading. Laying on the snow, the damp cold seeping into her clothing, Alex looked up at the sky.

"What did you see?"

"Orion and Sir Oliver. By the river. Something was in the river. They were…" Alex stopped speaking. What had been in the river? Something? Someone?

"You are with Orion, the dragon? Who is Sir Oliver? You have not told him about your magic, have you?" Meredith stepped over the stool, looming over Alex, one hand pushing against her shoulder, keeping her on the ground.

Alex shuddered at the contact, but did not shy away. "Orion is the dragon, yes. But he is not wholly dragon now, he is…only part. Sir Oliver is a friend from his childhood. We are on a quest." Alex edged from beneath Meredith's hand. "And no, I have not told him about my magic. I have not told *anyone* else about it."

"We? You are traveling with them? You are no longer at the castle?"

"No, I am no longer at the castle. We are traveling by a river…" The river in her vision, it was the same river they were traveling by today, at this moment, away from her dream and the meadow. Alex brushed off Meredith's hand. "I must get back…"

"No, you must tell me what you saw, what was in your vision."

"I told you what I saw: Orion and Sir Oliver trying to pull something from the river. No, I think it was someone…" Alex stared at the cooling pot of water, steam no longer writhing upward. Though its warmth had melted the snow to expose the damp, yellow grass beneath it, the snow was beginning to stick to the bottom.

"But what did you feel?" Meredith grabbed her should again, shaking her slightly.

"I couldn't breathe. The steam, it was too much." Alex pulled away again. "I have to get back…"

There was no more steam coming from the pot; it had completely cooled and ice formed on the surface of the water.

Meredith lunged for her shoulder again, but Alex dodged it, avoiding her hand, pushing herself to her feet. She continued to stare at the pot. "I have to get back…"

Someone shook her, called out to her. But Meredith's hands were at her sides and she stood a yard away, Alex backing away from her…

CHAPTER EIGHT

Alex awoke with a start, taking a deep breath, grabbing at the hands shaking her.

"I'm awake! I'm awake!" She could feel the warmth of the sun above her and the grass beneath her. Her head ached, and something sticky ran down her cheek. "Ouch!"

"Alex!" Orion held her, pressing her to his chest, rocking her gently. Alex could see Oliver standing behind him, bent over, hands braced against his knees and his eyes wide.

Gently, Orion set her back on the ground. Soft hands brushed at her cheek. "Ow!" Alex gasped at the pain, shrinking from his touch.

"Shh." Orion smoothed her hair back. "You hit your head and cut yourself when you fell from your horse. Let me check the damage."

Alex nodded and whimpered, biting her lip. Tears started at the corners of her eyes.

"Don't move. I know it hurts. Shh." Orion whispered the words near her ear. "It is a bit nasty. It will leave a scar. The cut runs from your temple to your ear."

Oliver stepped forward, pressing a white cloth toward Orion. "Here. Put pressure on it. You need to stop the bleeding."

Orion took the cloth. "Thank you."

Alex could see the white cloth move to her temple, blocking her sight. "No."

"Alex…" Orion's voice was hoarse.

"Orion! I can stop it myself." Her voice was low and shaky, but she struggled to sit up, ignoring the jarring pain that pierced her temple. "Help me up."

Oliver snorted. "How do you plan to stop the bleeding?" He paced away then came near again, his feet slamming at the ground, any sympathy evaporating with each step. "He is costing us time, Orion. We should never have brought him with us. Though," Oliver snorted again, "now I know why you insisted he come."

Alex stopped listening to Oliver, stopped feeling Orion's arm where it wound around her, supporting her back. She found the bubble of cold inside her, made it grow until she could no longer feel the warmth of the sun on her face and her fingers chilled. Slowly, she moved the cold to the pain, feeling it numb her temple. Then, the numbness left, and she was cold, cold like the snow in the meadow, cold like the ice that covered the turrets of the mountain castle. Piercing cold streaking from her temple to her ear.

The healing completed, she fought the cold, pushed it back, back to her center. She rebuilt the barrier, holding it in check, shuddering at the strength it took away. In the end, she huddled next to Orion, shivering while the sun beat down upon them.

Orion ran his hands up and down her arms, chafing warmth back into them. "Fetch a blanket." He barked the order harshly over his shoulder. When Oliver did not move, Orion growled. "Fetch…a…blanket!"

Oliver moved then, a flicker of black against the green of the grass. He threw the blanket to Orion, keeping a good distance between them.

Wrapping the blanket around Alex, Orion tucked it tightly to her shivering form. He pulled her to his chest, rocking her once again.

Teeth chattering, Alex buried her nose into his neck, feeling him shudder against her. "S-s-sorry."

"'S'okay. It's just…your nose is freezing."

"D-d-did the b-b-bleeding s-s-stop?"

Orion checked her temple, his fingers a welcoming stab of heat against her frigid skin. "Just a little scar left."

Oliver sucked in an audible breath. Alex tried to turn her head to see him, but Orion kept her tucked snug to his chest. "Wait until you're warm."

"He…he healed the wound?" Oliver staggered to the ground, sitting heavily near them. "H-h-how?"

Orion watched his friend. Alex could see the burning light in his eyes. The dragon was close, but maybe not too close to the surface. His breath was hot, fire-hot to her cold.

"Orion?" Oliver watched them from a short distance.

The heat that Orion gave off warmed Alex quickly, and she sighed as the last of the cold seeped away. "I'm fine now." She patted Orion on the chest. "I can explain to Oliver."

Orion turned his eyes to her face, and Alex could see the dragon there, just below the surface. Alex had been wrong; the dragon was too close to the surface.

Alex smirked, whispering to Orion. "You need to go cool down."

Orion nodded once, gently arranging her on the ground, then stood and moved away to the shade of the trees, keeping his back to them. Alex watched his chest move in and out; he took great gulps of air, his hands running frantically through the fire of his hair.

Alex turned back to look at Oliver. Oliver stared back at her, his mouth slightly open, his breath loud and his eyes wide.

"I have magic." She spoke low, keeping the tone gentle. Meredith would not be happy that she was sharing that secret with yet another person. Alex felt a little thrill work its way over her nerves; it felt good to do something Meredith would not approve.

"Oh." Oliver's mouth formed the sound slowly.

"That's why Orion wanted me to come."

Oliver shook his head. "Not the only reason... unnatural."

Alex frowned. "What are you talking about?" She knew most people were scared of magic, but to call it unnatural? She supposed it was logical, but...

At a snort from behind, she turned to see Orion walking back to them, much calmer now. She could see only the glint of turquoise in his eyes; the fire had been doused. He squatted next to Alex. "I understand what he means."

Oliver flushed, his cheeks turning pink, like a mild sunburn. "I saw you. You...you..." Oliver turned his head away.

Alex still frowned. "What did you see?"

Orion laughed. Alex couldn't help but smile at the sound. It seemed to fill the air around them.

Oliver shook his head again. "I saw." He jabbed a finger in Orion's direction.

"Yes, you saw. But you don't yet know all of Alex's secrets." Orion stood up, holding one hand out to help Alex stand.

Oliver stood and stalked away, ignoring them.

Raising one brow, Alex ignored the outstretched hand and stood up on her own, brushing leaves and dirt from her clothing.

Orion sighed. "Ally..." he spoke softly.

Alex pursed her lips before speaking tightly, keeping her voice low. "Ally is not here; she's back at the castle in my closet. Only Alex is here."

Orion watched her. "There is no difference."

"Of course there is a difference."

Orion glared at Alex, leaning down to put his face close to hers. "There is no difference."

Alex flinched, but did not back away. "I refuse to be intimidated. Especially by you." She took a deep breath. "There is a big difference between Ally and Alex. You should know that."

Orion smiled. "And therein lies your problem. Ally would not be intimidated, either." Orion moved away, looking around and raising his voice. "I think we should make camp here. We could all do with a rest, I think."

"Yes." Oliver agreed with Orion for the first time since leaving the castle. "I think we should stay here until morning." The two young men walked to the horses, retrieving packs and satchels. Oliver tied his horse off to a tree; Orion tied his and

Alex's to another nearby. Saddles were removed and blankets laid out to dry.

The horses shook, their tails swatting the air and the flies. The white mare whinnied, and Orion ran his hands over her back.

Alex stood silent, the blanket draped over her shoulders, one corner trailing on the ground behind her. She stared at the river, the large jagged rock sitting at the shoreline, the small copse of trees swaying slightly in the breeze on the far shore.

This is where her vision had taken place. Just at this spot along the river.

Moving forward, she edged toward the rushing water, dropping the blanket to the ground. Her eyes skimmed its churning surface. What had Oliver and Orion been after? Closing her eyes, Alex thought of the vision, recreating it in her mind. She could smell lemongrass and a hint of sage again. The flavors burst into her mouth, their scents filling her nose. She shivered again, wishing she'd kept the blanket.

The lemongrass grew stronger, until it was everything, the very air she breathed.

The scene unfolded. Orion in the river, the water swirling and rushing at his calves. Oliver stretching out his arm, holding him to the shore.

Alex forced her vision away from Orion and Oliver, forced them to the river. Red. There was a flash of red in the river. A head and an arm. Someone was in the river, the current sweeping them past.

A scream rent the air.

Opening her eyes, Alex scanned the river. She saw the flash of red, a head, an arm...there *was* someone in the river!

"Orion!" Alex gasped out, running toward the river bank. "Help!" She stumbled a bit on a stone, catching herself, before pitching forward to her knees in the soft mud. "There's someone in the river!"

From the corner of her sight, Alex saw Orion drop the pack he was carrying and rush to the river, Oliver right behind him.

"There is someone there!" Alex struggled to her regain her feet, slipping in the muck, pointing with one shaky finger.

"I see!" Orion plunged into the river, nearly losing his balance on the rocks, the current pushing at him.

Oliver grabbed his arm, pulling him back. "You can't reach him!"

Alex was now standing, watching the figure in the water. She could see the red, and long blond hair. It was not a "him"; it was a "her".

Without a thought, Alex waded further into the river.

"Alex! No!" Orion struggled with Oliver, thrusting him back, and his friend fell to the ground.

Waist-deep in the rushing water, she fought a losing battle with the current. Alex let herself be pulled in, lifting her feet from the riverbed. The trees twirled by, a dizzying dance across her eyes. Alex saw a quick flash of red to her left and reached out, grasping, searching with her fingers.

A cold, wet hand reached her and Alex wound her fingers around it, pulling. Two sets of fingers entwined. Her shoulder wrenched, and she gasped in pain. Water rushed into her mouth and nose. She couldn't breathe. Her lungs filled with water. Alex coughed, choked and cried out.

Dimly, she heard shouting. "Alex! Alex! Ally!"

Spitting out the water, she shoved her face skyward, into the air. Turning to her right, Alex saw Orion running along the bank, keeping pace with her and the current. She pulled on the red figure, managing to get it close enough to wind one arm around it, anchoring it to her. Kicking her feet, Alex aimed for the bank.

Orion entered the water again when Alex was within reach, grasping, pulling, sliding them to the bank. Oliver was there to help now, heaving the sodden, red-clad figure out of the water to relative safety. Orion didn't let go of Alex.

Alex coughed, water churning out of her lungs, lunging to her knees beside Orion. She crawled to the figure in sodden red and smacked it on the back and it spasmed. A tangled blonde head rose up, looking from one to the other to the third. Light blue eyes swept over them. Alex could hear a gasping breath, but couldn't tell who it came from. Even Orion and Oliver were breathing hard.

The first person who spoke was Orion. "Your parents would have killed me." He gasped out, punching Alex lightly on the shoulder.

Alex shook her head." I think (gasp) that they know (shudder) me well enough now (long breath out.) Besides, I don't think they are in any position to be killing anyone at the moment."

"Nope." Orion was still shaking his head. "They would have found a way to kill me. Or Gwennie. She's fully capable." Orion gasped his own breath in and sat up, pulling Alex farther from the water. She lay back on the warm grass, closing her eyes to the sun, and tried to calm her still-labored breaths. "I'm supposed to be watching out for you."

Opening one eye, Alex glared at Orion. "Why would you be watching over me for my parents? They don't even know I came with you and Sir Oliver." She rose up on her elbows to stare Orion in the face.

"You're the one who said they knew you well enough. They knew you would want to come. I am quite sure they would expect me to watch out for you." Orion met Alex's angry gaze with his own calm one.

Alex snorted, and decided to ignore Orion's misguided rantings. Instead she looked to the blonde in red.

She was obviously a lady. Her gown was deep red velvet, trimmed in dark cream lace. Alex could tell that the gown was expensive. She had been trained by Gwennie to recognize such; there was no sense performing for someone who could not afford to pay.

The girl's blonde hair fell in sodden curls down her back. Her feet were bare; her shoes likely lost to the rushing current of the river. She was young; Alex thought she might be just a bit older than she.

"Are you okay?" Alex asked the question and the two young men turned to look at the young woman together.

The blonde nodded. She was on her hands and knees in the muddy part of the bank just before it became the river, shuddering and gasping. "Yes..."

Her voice was soft and well mannered.

Definitely a lady, thought Alex.

CHAPTER NINE

The young lady sat back, arranging her wet skirts around her legs and flipping the tendrils of wet blonde hair back from her shoulders. She sat erect, her spine straight, her head up and chin out.

It was a pose Alex had recently become extremely familiar with and she had to hide her grimace in her shoulder.

"My name is Lady Chantelle de Sousong," she began, "and I thank you for retrieving me from the river." She nodded toward the still swirling and foaming water. "I am sure that I would have drowned had you not pulled me out."

The three nodded, staying silent, watching, waiting.

Lady Chantelle swallowed, taking a deep breath of air into her lungs. She coughed a bit, one hand to her chest. "My father will be eternally grateful and will reward you handsomely."

The three nodded again.

"My father is the Lord of Chateaux Sousong. I think you will find him overjoyed at my return."

The three nodded once more, glancing quickly between themselves. Alex decided to speak up, asking the question all three of them wanted answered. "How did you wind up in the river?"

The blonde took another long breath. "That is a very long story, and I would like to be dry before I begin. Might I be taken to your holding and offered something dry to wear? Perhaps something warm to drink?"

The three looked at each other again. It was Orion who spoke this time. "We don't have a holding per se, not nearby anyway – there is only the three of us and our horses. We are on a quest and were about to make camp when Alex saw you in the river and rushed in to save you. I am not sure any of us have anything we can offer you to wear-"

Alex cut in. "I have something in my satchel. Let's finish making camp."

Oliver snorted. "Of course, you do." The words were whispered low; Alex barely heard them, but decided to ignore them for now. Maybe Orion could explain to her what Oliver was going on about.

Orion stood. "I will gather wood for a fire. Oliver, why don't you take care of the horses? My Lady," he bowed regally to the blonde, "Alex will provide you with something dry to wear."

"Please," the lady said, extending one pale hand gracefully, "call me only by my first name, Chantelle. Saving my life has earned you that right." Her smile was regal.

Alex wanted to cringe, but suppressed the reaction, choosing instead to stand and fetch her satchel. Lady Chantelle's smile was more royal than her own, and Alex had been practicing for months now.

Orion took her offered hand and nodded over it, helping her to stand, before walking toward the forest to gather wood. Oliver started walking back to the tethered horses and dropped packs. Alex retrieved her satchel from her horse. It took her little time to return, and she knelt on the ground near Lady Chantelle, searching through it.

"Aha!" Alex pulled the light woolen gown she'd worn over her trousers to escape the castle. Though the fabric was plain and undyed, its quality was the best, the stitching tight and even, the weave almost felted. Alex handed the gown to Lady Chantelle then dug through her satchel for the proper undergarments she'd brought along just in case they were needed. "I apologize for their rumpled condition, but I rather had to cram them in here. It may be a bit short on you."

Lady Chantelle frowned at the offering, stealing a confused glance at Alex before accepting the dry clothing. Balancing carefully in the water-logged gown, she looked around. "Thank you."

Alex looked around as well. The area was quite open, save for the dense forest that rose like a planted pole fence a hundred feet from the river's edge. Orion tramped along its edge, picking up dry twigs and branches for the fire. Oliver led the horses from their original tethered positions to their new camp.

"Let me arrange a place for you to change." Taking the blankets from the packs, Alex strung them up at the forest's edge, tying them to thick branches to create a curtained area.

"Thank you, again." Lady Chantelle nodded her head at Alex when they passed, then entered the makeshift changing room; Alex could hear the rustle of clothing.

Ignoring the sounds, Alex gathered stones for the fire ring, placing them in the middle of the clearing, a safe distance from the trees and closer to the water. Orion brought the branches and twigs to the ring, and dropped them in a haphazard pile next to it.

"What if Oliver recognizes the dress?"

Alex looked up to see Orion staring down at her, one thumb pointing toward Lady Chantelle behind the blankets. She snorted. "He will think I stole it."

Orion shook his head, glancing toward the curtained area when a squeal of frustration came out of it. Alex turned her head to look as well.

The blankets billowed out slightly from the movement inside. The barest top of a blond head could be seen above the curtains, bobbing up and down.

"My lady?" Orion called out, his voice tentative.

They heard another squeal. Oliver joined them, their meager supply of food in hand. "What's happening?"

Alex smirked and muffled a giggle behind her hand. "I would say Lady Chantelle is having difficulty with the ties of her gown."

Oliver glared down at Alex. "'tis not polite to make fun of one's betters."

Alex glared back. "I am not making fun."

"Right!" Orion interrupted them. "How do we offer help?" He was looking down at Alex.

"Orion! We cannot offer a peasant boy to tie her laces! 'tis most unseemly. She will think we are rogues of the worst sort!" Oliver placed their food on the ground next to the pile of wood.

"Oh?" Orion twisted his lips. "Are you going to offer to help her? Might that not be interpreted as a roguish act?"

Oliver flushed, his cheeks turning a dull red from jaw to hairline. "Of course not," he whispered, frantic, "but you are a prince, and your actions are above reproach."

Orion raised his brows at that, but did not have a chance to respond. Lady Chantelle had approached them, her hands holding the bodice of the gown to her front.

"You are a prince?" She stared at Orion, mouth open in a not-quite-attractive manner.

Orion bowed. "Prince Orion of Paixor." He smirked, glancing to the side at Alex, "Though I am not in line for a throne."

Lady Chantelle curtseyed and almost fell; she was still trying to hold up the bodice of her wet gown.

Alex bit back her laughter, making a choking sound in the back of her throat instead.

Orion stood from his bow and pushed her, setting her off balance.

Oliver rolled his eyes. "One would not know it from the way you act."

Orion lunged at Oliver, making to push him as well, but Oliver dodged his advance, his bark of laughter echoing in the otherwise stillness.

Alex smiled. She discovered that she liked Oliver when he was like this. "Lady Chantelle, if I may offer my assistance." Alex held up one hand when she made to protest. "I can untie your laces at the bottom, and loosen them. You should then be able to work them loose to remove your wet gown."

Lady Chantelle considered Alex for a moment before nodding and turning her back to her.

"You will also find," Alex grunted a little at the wet ribbon, "that the gown I gave you has no such lacing to cause you difficulty. There are buttons on the front, covered by a layer of fabric to hide them." Alex continued tugging at the now untied ribbon, loosening the lower back of the dress. "There you are. That should work."

"Thank you." Stiffly, Lady Chantelle walked back to the strung up blankets, her hands clutching at the front of her gown in case it had been loosened enough to fall.

Oliver snorted, shaking his head. "For the way you are, you know a lot about undoing lady's laces."

"What do you mean, for the way I am?" Alex crossed her arms across her chest, glaring at Oliver.

"Oliver..." Orion's voice was low and harsh.

"What?" Oliver rounded on Orion. "I cannot believe that you...you..." He waved his hands around his head wildly.

Orion's lips twisted and he braced his fists against his hips, leaning toward Oliver. "You cannot believe I... what?" His voice remained low, but Alex recognized the anger laced in the words.

Alex looked from one to the other, confused.

"You know..." Oliver waved his hands between Orion and Alex, "with *him*." Oliver pointed his finger at Alex.

Alex finally understood what Oliver was getting at--and gasped. "B...b...but... n...n...no!"

Orion glanced at Alex, and snickered. "Not yet at any rate..."

Alex smacked him on the arm--hard enough to make him wince.

Oliver turned green.

Orion snickered again. "Part of the problem for him," Orion felt the need to explain to Alex, leaning down close, "is that you're a boy!"

Alex glared at Orion. She could tell by the way Orion's lips were quivering that he was trying not to laugh. "If you dare say 'I told you so,' I'll...I'll..."

"You'll what?" Orion wasn't even bothering to hide his laughter anymore; it was spilling out, filling the space between Alex's stuttering words.

Alex turned her back on him, facing an even greener-faced Oliver. Taking a deep breath, Alex decided it was time to come clean at least about one other secret. She couldn't have Oliver thinking that about Orion! No wonder he was so twitchy!

She took a deep breath. "Oliver, I'm not a boy."

Oliver stared, his mouth agape.

"Really, I'm not." Alex nodded her head at him, willing him to believe her.

Oliver frowned. "I want proof."

"Proof?" It was Orion who asked the question, the word coming out a bit strangled, like there was something caught in his throat.

"Yes." Oliver was nodding his head now. "I want proof."

Alex made to speak but was stopped by Orion.

"No. You'll just have to believe it."

Alex rounded back to Orion. "I can prove I'm a girl!"

Orion raised a brow.

"I can!"

"But you're not going to. He's only going to accept definitive proof, and I won't let you."

"Huh?" Alex flushed when she realized what Orion meant. "Oh. Right." Cheeks pink, she turned back to Oliver. "I guess you'll just have to take my word for it."

Orion snickered. "And mine. After all, if I'm a prince, my word is all that should be necessary, eh?" He glared at Oliver.

Oliver did not look happy, but he nodded stiffly.

Lady Chantelle joined the group, holding up the hem of the dress in her hands. It was a bit too long for her and a bit tight in the hips and shoulder, but it was dry and covered her.

Alex glanced over to the curtained area. The red gown lay on the ground, a small pool of water gathering around it, muddying the dirt. Sighing, Alex walked over to the dress, picked it up and shook it. She hung it over a thin branch, making sure it didn't touch the ground. She smoothed the wrinkles, arranging the dress so that it would dry best. When she turned to pick up the rest of the wet clothing, she found Orion there, the items already in his hands.

"Thank you." Alex turned and performed the same procedures, only this time, wringing as much water out of them before arranging them on the branch. She hadn't dared wring out the red velvet – she knew that would ruin the soft nap of the fabric.

"Why did you do that?"

Alex looked up at Orion, surprised at his question. "Do what?"

"Pick up her things." He glared at the sodden clothing.

"Why not?" She shrugged, smiling when he let out a rushed sigh.

"Lady Chantelle could have done that herself."

Alex snickered. "You're supposed to just call her by her first name. You earned it, remember?"

"No. You earned it." Orion straightened, shifting on his feet and crossing his arms. "Why?" This time the word was clipped.

Alex sighed. "Do you really think she knows what to do with wet clothing?"

Orion huffed. "That is not the point..."

Alex placed one hand on his arm; Orion looked down at it. "That is precisely the point, Orion. I am a gypsy, the servant in this group. It is what I know to do, and I should be the one to do it."

"But you aren't..." Orion whispered, his eyes meeting hers.

"I am to them. Really Orion, 'tis what I am inside, no matter who my parents are. I was raised a gypsy, and I am not ashamed of it." She patted his arm and turned to walk back to Oliver and Lady Chantelle. "I will get the fire lit and supper started."

Orion didn't follow right away, but stood quietly by the trees, staring at the opposite bank of the river.

CHAPTER TEN

The fire was bright and hot, and the four sat around, drinking and eating their meager meal. Oliver's provisions were getting sparse. Alex had suggested once that they refill their provisions, but a glare from Oliver had immediately stopped her speech. She was not sure what his problem was, but Orion had shot her a cautious look and she had let it drop.

Now though, Alex peeked at Lady Chantelle. The lady was having difficulty swallowing the stale biscuit and dried meat, and was following the food with great gulps of weak tea.

Alex chewed her own food slowly, sipping bits of tea into her mouth to let it soak into the food. It was not much for taste, but is satisfied one's hunger. Between the biscuits and meat, and the dried fruit they ate in the morning, the fare was relatively healthy, if sparse.

Lady Chantelle sighed and placed her plate on the ground by her feet. "Thank you for the meal."

"You are welcome." Orion answered, since Oliver had his mouth full of biscuit. "Are you ready to tell us your story, now?"

"I believe so, yes." Lady Chantelle nodded her head firmly then twisted her fingers together in her lap. "It all began months--perhaps even a year--ago, when my father was visited by a lord who was interested in having my hand for marriage.

He plied my father with gifts--silk, spices, livestock--anything that my father mentioned in passing arrived on our doorstep."

Lady Chantelle took a deep breath, her eyes wandering to the river. "My father was quite flattered, of course, but he was not sure that I would agree. He had promised me long ago that I would have a say in who I married, and he kept explaining this to the lord."

She took a breath, raising her chin. "But the lord never spoke to me. Not once. Never was *I* brought a gift, even a token that showed he knew that I existed. And so I told my father to refuse his suit."

"Then, there came a storm. And during the storm, men came to the castle. I don't know how they did it, but they must have come to my room in the night, while I was asleep, and stolen me away. When I awoke, I was on a palette of blankets in a round, stone room. There was a single window to the outside. Sunlight came through the window, so I looked out."

"I found that I was in a tower. Not an overly tall tower, but still, a tower. I would have been killed had I tried to jump from the window. There was a trap door in the floor of the room, but I could not raise it. I think it was locked from below."

"When this lord finally came to visit me, he demanded that I agree to the marriage. I refused. He told me that I could rot in the tower, and that my father would never know that I had died. No one would be able to get me in the tower."

"I told him that my father had brave men who served him that would come for me. He laughed. It was a horrible sound, echoing through the room. He sneered at me. They will never get past the dragon, he told me."

At the word dragon, Oliver looked up from his meal, brown eyes wide, and turned to Lady Chantelle. Alex could see the light of excitement in his eyes.

"The tower was guarded by a fierce dragon, a dragon that would kill on sight, or so the lord said. There was no way that I could get out, and even if I did, the dragon would surely kill me." Lady Chantelle was crying now, her tears leaking down her pale cheeks and dripping off her chin.

"Then how did you escape from the tower?" Oliver ignored his supper, his plate lurching to the side, his last half biscuit precariously balanced on the edge.

"Well. The dragon, she...she was being forced by the lord to do this. He has some power over her. I saw him one day when I was watching from the window. He rode up on his horse with his men behind, and he held something up to the dragon and spoke to her. He told her that he still had "the egg", and that if she obeyed him then he would give it back to her."

Oliver bit his lip, nearly bouncing on the rock he sat on. His excitement crackled in the air around him. "This is it. This is the story that I was told back in Paixor." Oliver reached out and grabbed his friend's arm. "Orion, we are almost there!"

"Oliver," Orion's voice was low and calm, "this dragon is being forced to do this horrible deed. We must reconsider..."

"Never! They are evil and I will hunt this one down and destroy it!" Oliver's plate went flying, his arms waving in the air around his head. "We are almost there!"

Lady Chantelle rose to her feet as well, regal and still next to Oliver's frantic waving and dancing. "Please. You must not harm the beast. She is the reason that I escaped. She helped me, despite what she was forced to do."

"No. It is an animal. It does not think in such terms." Oliver stood toe-to-toe with Lady Chantelle.

"The dragon helped me from the tower. She flew to the window and let me on her back. It is not her fault I fell from her back. You must not hurt her!"

"You speak of it like it is a person!" Oliver spat the words. Lady Chantelle wiped a delicate finger across her cheek.

Orion leaned forward, placing his own plate with his remaining supper, on the ground, leaning his elbows on his knees. "Oliver, you must listen to Lady Chantelle. She is the one with experience with this dragon. If she thinks that the dragon is not a menace, then we should believe her."

Oliver turned on his friend, is hand slicing through the air above the fire. "You have been trying to convince me that I am wrong since before we left Vreden Castle. This is just more of the same from you."

"Yes, I have been trying to talk sense into you since I joined you on this journey. I do not believe that all dragons are evil. I think that you are wrong to assume that this one needs to be killed. And now," Orion raised his voice to keep Oliver silent when he made to speak, "here is proof. This dragon helped Lady Chantelle escape from her prison."

"Proof? This is not proof. This is the fancy of a girl!"

Lady Chantelle gasped. "A girl! You speak like I am a child telling fairy tales!"

"It sounds like a fairy tale to me. There is no common sense to your story."

Orion rubbed his hands over his face, staring at his friend between his fingers. "Oliver. Listen to yourself, please."

"I am. And I am the only one making sense."

"No, you are not!" Orion stood up, his hands tight fists at his sides.

Alex sighed, swallowing the bit of biscuit in her mouth, slowly so it would not catch and make her choke. "Are you two going to fight?"

Oliver and Orion both looked down at her. Lady Chantelle looked, too, but her face was apprehensive, rather than angry.

"No." Orion spoke first, looking away to the sky. "We aren't going to fight."

"Yes, we are." Oliver spoke quickly, his words running over Orion's.

"No, we are not, because I am ending this conversation." Orion turned from the fire and walked away, his back rigid and his head up. He called back, waving one arm in the air. "Do not worry if I am not back before dark."

Alex watched him walk away. She knew what he was going to do--transform and take to the sky, likely in search of this female dragon. She wanted to go with him, but she had not been asked. She placed her own plate on the ground, no longer hungry. She thought of the female dragon, of the egg that Lady Chantelle had mentioned, and of the object used to make the dragon comply with this "lord".

Toeing the edge of her plate, she watched the stale biscuit slide along the surface. Lady Chantelle and Oliver's plates had been abandoned, as well as Orion's. Stooping, she picked them all up, crumbling the biscuits and scattering the bits by the river for the birds. She washed the plates, drying them with a small cloth kept for that purpose.

Avoiding Oliver, she carefully packed the rest of the food and the plates away in a large satchel.

Oliver paced near the forest line, muttering to himself and waving his hands about. Every so often, Alex could hear an angry expletive burst from his mouth and he'd shake a fist at something--probably someone--imaginary standing in front of him.

Lady Chantelle sat next to the fire, staring into the flames. Her hands were primly folded in her lap, her spine straight, her golden hair hanging down her back, the tangles catching on each other.

"Lady Chantelle, would you like a brush for your hair?"

The young lady turned to look at Alex, a slight look of surprise on her face. "Have you a brush?"

Alex nodded, smiling at the lady's surprise, and walked to the small satchel that lay on the ground near her horse. She retrieved the brush, as well as a small mirror and a pair of silver hair combs.

"Thank you." Lady Chantelle accepted the gifts and began to brush her hair. It was clear to Alex that she was not used to performing this task herself--she had started brushing from the top of her head, and was simply making the tangles worse.

"Would you like me to brush your hair for you? I am not inexperienced in the task." Alex offered from a few feet away. Lady Chantelle always looked uncomfortable when speaking to Alex.

"Where would you have brushed a lady's hair?"

Alex felt a flush of anger heat her cheeks. "It is not just lady's that require their hair to be brushed. The woman who raised me had long hair; I brushed it for her frequently."

Lady Chantelle let the brush sink to her lap, and looked over Alex from head to toe. "Who was this woman?"

"She was a gypsy. She took care of me. We travelled a lot."

"Oh." Lady Chantelle looked back to the fire, and began brushing her hair again.

Alex sighed. "You are making the tangles worse. You will have nothing but knots in the ends when you brush that way." She spoke softly.

Lady Chantelle did not stop her brushing. "It is unseemly for me to have you brush my hair."

Alex crossed her arms across her chest. "There is no one here to see me brush your hair."

"I will know."

"It would be that horrible, just to think of it?"

"I am a lady. I must always think in terms of what is seemly and decorous. It is what a lady does." Lady Chantelle had the brush stuck in a particularly bad tangle, and winced while tugging hard at the brush.

Alex took a deep, steadying breath. If the lady didn't want help, Alex wouldn't force it on her. She turned back to the horses, making sure they were tied snug to their trees and that they had water for the night.

Dark was settling over the camp when Alex finished all the chores. Lady Chantelle had only sat and brushed her hair; Sir Oliver had paced away most of the evening.

And Orion wasn't back yet.

Alex scanned the sky, looking for a darker shape against the black of the night sky, but saw nothing. Clouds hid even the stars and moon from view. The only light was from the fire.

She gathered more wood and stacked it near the fire, but far enough away that it would not be accidentally set alight. Then she gathered the blankets and set up their beds, ringing them close to the fire for warmth and protection, using a spare blanket for Lady Chantelle's.

Oliver still muttered to himself at the edges of the firelight.

Lady Chantelle still tried to brush her hair, wincing at every knot she encountered.

Alex sighed, wishing only that Orion would get back soon.

CHAPTER ELEVEN

The first person Alex saw in the morning was Orion. His head lay near hers, his eyes closed in sleep, his mouth relaxed. She studied his face a moment, wondering when he had gotten back and if anyone else had been awake then. He shifted and his hair, the auburn locks curling slightly, fell over his forehead and over his eyes. Alex quelled the urge to brush his hair back, instead sitting up and looking at the others.

Oliver lay on his back, as usual, soft snoring erupting fitfully from his sleeping form. His blanket was draped over his chest, rising and falling with his breaths. His black tunic, the silver-threaded crest of Paixor right side up, was draped over his satchel, his left hand clutching its hem.

Lady Chantelle lay curled on her side, her hands folded neatly beneath her pink cheek. She did not snore; in fact, Alex could barely tell the lady was breathing at all, except that her hair, which fell in snarled masses over her face, puffed out a bit at regular intervals.

The fire was down to glowing embers and the sun was rising above the horizon, lightening the air around the camp. The horses shuffled, munching the leaves within their reach.

Alex turned her gaze back to Orion and found him watching her, propped up on one elbow.

"Good morning." He spoke softly, smiling.

Alex smiled back. "Good morning. Feeling better?"

Orion glanced to the ever-lightening sky. "A little. I still feel a little..." He swallowed and shrugged.

"I think I know how you feel." Alex watched his gaze return to her face. "Sir Oliver is so...so stubborn about this. And I know you like to fly..."

"Yeah. That's the best part, you know." Orion grinned at her. "That and generating heat for you, when you get...cold. And it would be much easier getting a fire lit if I was able to just...you know..." he mimed blowing fire, "poof."

Alex grinned back. "Much easier that way."

Orion lay back, staring straight up, one hand behind his head. "What do you think will happen when we find the dragon? Do you think Oliver will actually destroy it? Or do you think we'll be able to persuade him not to?"

"I'm not sure how much persuading I'll be able to do, but I plan to try my best."

"Hmmph."

"I mean," Alex poked Orion on the shoulder, "it's not like he listens to me. You're the only one he listens to, even if it is only on occasion."

Orion sighed. "I suppose." He craned his head back, looking at her upside down and half crooked. "I just thought that having someone else back up my claims would help. Lady Chantelle is a stranger; it's not like I could have planned this or anything."

"I think he's just determined to do this. He set out to kill a dragon and gain glory, like you told me, and he isn't going to turn back now." Alex pushed off her blanket and stood up, folding it deftly into a small bundle, ready to be put into her satchel.

"I suppose. I just wish..." Orion stood and gathered his own blankets, folding his not quite so neatly. Alex took it from him and refolded it, then stacked it on top of hers.

"I know. Let's get the fire going and breakfast started."

Orion groaned. "Tea and dried fruit?"

Alex crossed her eyes at him. "What else?"

Orion eyed the river. "I could try catching some fish."

"You could try. Have you anything to catch them with? A line and a hook?" Alex retrieved some wood and laid it in a pyramid over the graying embers.

Orion grimaced. "No. I didn't think to pack anything like that. I guess I figured I'd have him talked around after a week and we'd be back at the castle." He struck two pieces of flint together, directing the sparks at the tinder Alex had placed beneath the wood. The tinder was slightly damp and did not light.

Alex glanced at Lady Chantelle and Oliver. The two were still sound asleep. "Here," she whispered, "allow me."

Orion stopped tapping the flint and watched Alex.

Alex concentrated on the tinder, pulling at the cold inside, thinking flame and heat. The tinder began to smoke and soon caught fire. Smiling, Alex shivered. "That wasn't so bad."

"But you're cold now."

"Only a bit. I'll warm up soon."

Orion frowned at her. "I don't like that you get so cold when you use your magic."

Alex glanced at their sleeping companions. Though Oliver had been told about her magic, Lady Chantelle had not. "There's nothing I can do about it. It's what happens. I've explained before, it's like a cold well inside of me."

"It can't be right though. I would think your magic wouldn't disable you like that."

"Maybe that's just the price I have to pay to use it. I do not believe that we get anything for free. We must work for it." Alex shivered again, rubbing her hands over her arms. The tinder had lit the wood, and more smoke was drifting up, but there was still little heat.

"Come here." Orion held out his arm.

Alex looked at his arm a moment before moving closer to let it drape over her shoulder. The heat of it felt wonderful, and she let it seep into her. Slowly, the shivers stopped and she was warm again. She shifted beneath his arm, glancing at the two sleeping forms.

"Thanks."

Orion said nothing but sighed and removed his arm.

The two watched the wood catch light and the fire grow. Minutes passed; Oliver groaned in his sleep and turned to his side.

Orion laughed. "Well, that's the signal that he'll be awake soon. I'll fetch the water for his morning brew. You dig out the dried fruit; see if you can find a way to make it a bit more palatable this morning."

Alex laughed in return, standing to search the satchel for the fruit. Maybe...yes. There was the fruit, and the biscuits; if only she had a bit of honey...

Orion had the water set over the fire. "Any ideas?"

"I wish we had some honey."

"Honey?"

Alex nodded. "I could crumble the biscuits and put it with the fruit in some water and make a bit of a porridge. Honey would make it sweeter." Alex dug through the satchel for the biscuits.

"Do you have something to put it in?"

"The porridge?" Alex's voice was muffled; her head was half hidden by the satchel.

Orion snorted softly. "No, the honey. I can see about getting some."

Alex looked up from her search, the tin of biscuits in her hand. "I think there might be a small pot in my bag, over there." She nodded in the direction of her pack.

Orion found the pot, and with a quick salute, disappeared into the forest.

Smiling, humming just a little under her breath, Alex crumbled four biscuits into a bit of water, added some dried fruit, and placed it on the fire to heat and soften. The water, for Oliver's morning brew, began to boil, and Alex watched the bubbles form on the bottom of the pot and rise to the surface, slowly at first, then faster.

Soon, the bubbles were bursting at the surface and it was ready.

Alex made the dark bitter drink for Oliver, setting it aside, wedged between two rocks, to cool. Stirring the pot of makeshift porridge, she glanced to Oliver.

Oliver was awake, staring at her.

"Good morning. Your brew is made." She nodded at the cooling pot.

Oliver grunted, squinting his eyes into the morning light. "Where's Orion?"

"He is off to see if he can find some honey."

"Honey?" Oliver struggled with his blanket, his stilted movements only serving to twist the fabric more tightly around his legs.

Alex observed this from half-averted eyes. She had learned the first morning of the quest to leave Oliver to his own actions in the morning. Only his brew seemed to bring him fully awake and cure him from being entirely too disgruntled.

"I am trying to make us a bit of porridge for breakfast." Alex stirred the pot again, checking to see if it needed more water. She added a bit, stirring it in carefully.

Oliver grunted again. His eyes were closed, but he had managed to escape from his blanket.

Alex fetched his thick tin mug from the satchel and carefully poured some of the black liquid into it. She set it beside Oliver. "Here is your morning cup. Mind, it is still hot."

Oliver nodded, grasping the mug's handle with a slightly unsteady hand. He sipped at the liquid, hissing at the heat.

"What is that?" Lady Chantelle sat up and stared at Oliver and his mug, her nose curled.

It was Alex who replied. "That is Sir Oliver's morning brew. It helps him to wake up. I have more water heating for our tea. It should be ready soon."

"What is in his brew?"

Alex sat back on her knees and looked at Lady Chantelle. "He told me it is made from a bean from a distant land. It is roasted and crushed and boiled in water. He has a sack of the grains in his pack."

Lady Chantelle nodded. "It does not smell very pleasant. I cannot imagine it tastes any better." She stood from her blankets, shaking out her skirts. Looking around at the makeshift camp, she sighed. "Where might I take my morning constitution?"

Alex stared at Lady Chantelle a moment before comprehension hit. "Oh. We usually just walk a bit into the forest, and...um...take care of things."

Lady Chantelle stared at Alex. "The forest? But there are animals in there." She looked askance at the barrier of trees beside their camp.

"There is privacy in the forest, as well. About the only private place available for such... activities." Alex continued stirring the pot of porridge.

"Do you have a cloth?"

Alex looked up from the pot. "A cloth?"

Lady Chantelle blushed. "For wiping...after."

Alex's mouth made an "O" but she said nothing. She glanced to the satchels. Was there a cloth that she could offer? "We usually just use leaves."

The look of horror on Lady Chantelle's face made Alex wince. "Okay, I'll find you something." Alex moved the pot of porridge from the flame so that it would not burn, and rummaged through her satchel. She found one of her tunics and offered it to Lady Chantelle. It was a soft fabric, and Alex didn't really want to offer it up for such a use, but she had nothing else.

"Here, it is not really for such use but..."

Alex was not able to finish her sentence. Lady Chantelle grabbed the offered tunic, muttered a muffled "thank you" and left for the forest.

Sighing, Alex turned back to the fire. Oliver was still sitting, his blankets piled beside him, sipping from his mug, his eyes closed tightly against the light. Lady Chantelle's blankets were also setting in a jumbled pile.

Picking up Lady Chantelle's blanket, Alex shook it out before folding it. Warily eyeing Oliver, she pondered taking his blankets to fold, but decided he was not quite awake enough for that yet.

"Where is Lady Chantelle?" Orion held the small pot in his hands, a light gold substance filling it to the brim.

Alex grinned at him. "Is that the honey?"

"Yes." Orion held out the pot. "One pot of honey at your disposal."

Giggling, Alex curtseyed, sweeping the blanket in her hand out as if it were a wide skirt. "Why thank you, kind sir."

Orion smiled. "You are getting good at that."

"Curtseying?"

Orion nodded.

Alex laughed out loud. "If 'twas a real skirt, I'd have been flat on my face in the dirt." She set the now-folded blanket with the others and accepted the honey, tasting it with one finger. "Mmm. Just what our porridge needs."

Alex placed the pot of porridge back on the flames and poured a bit of the honey in, stirring the thicker liquid in.

"Lady Chantelle?" Orion asked again.

"Taking care of her morning ritual."

"Her what?" Orion dropped dried leaves from a small sack into the pot of water to make tea.

Alex shot him a low look from beneath her lashes. "You know, the stuff we all have to do first thing in the morning?'

"Ah!" Orion nodded, stirring the leaves in the water. He removed the pot from the fire to set and steep. "Her ritual. Got it."

Sir Oliver only grunted at them over his mug.

CHAPTER TWELVE

Alex's stomach rumbled for lunch, but Oliver didn't want to stop.

"I don't like the looks of the terrain here. We need to keep going." Sir Oliver guided his mount around rocky outcrops and a deep gully. "We would be vulnerable here if we stopped."

"Vulnerable?" Lady Chantelle and the mare followed Sir Oliver, the horse automatically following the leader.

"We would have trouble running if someone came upon us. And they could easily block us in."

Lady Chantelle looked around, ignoring the horse beneath her. "Are you expecting someone to come upon us?"

"Nay." Orion spoke up. "He is just being overly cautious."

"Caution makes one safe, Orion."

Alex sighed and shifted behind Orion.

"You okay?" Orion whispered the words over his shoulder.

"I'm fine. I'm just hungry."

"Oliver, we are going to have to stop, soon. We need to eat, and the horses need to rest and drink water."

"We can wait."

They continued, single file, past the rocks, keeping the gully to their left, the horses plodding at a slow pace. The rocks grew sparse, the gully not as deep. The trail became wider, more even.

Olive stopped. "This is a road."

"Indeed." Oliver's abrupt stop was unexpected and Orion jerked the reins on his mount. Alex bumped her forehead on his shoulder. "Is that a problem?"

"Well, no. I suppose not." Oliver's horse danced and turned.

"I should hope not. I wouldn't mind seeing some other faces besides yours." Lady Chantelle lifted her chin.

"What does that mean?" Oliver frowned at the young woman.

"It means, I am quite tired of your grumpy visage." Lady Chantelle flapped the reins of the mare, urging her forward and past Sir Oliver.

"Grumpy?"

"Grumpy." Lady Chantelle and the mare pranced past Sir Oliver, followed by Orion and Alex together on his stallion. "And rude."

Oliver sat atop his horse, mouth agape, staring at them.

Lady Chantelle continued to lead, following the ever-widening road. Soon, it was flanked by green fields and meadows, ponds and distant barns, workers plowing.

It reminded her of past fields, and folks shying away from a dragon-Orion, before she knew he was Orion, when she thought he was just a regular dragon. It was not the same place, though, those fields had been near the mountains and the winter castle.

"I should be leading, not Lady Chantelle. That is why they are staring. They must think us ridiculous." Oliver's mutterings from the rear reached Alex and Orion.

Alex snickered.

Orion called back. "They might think *you* ridiculous, but not *me*."

"Har har." Oliver did not sound amused.

"This might be a good opportunity for you to ask about your dragon, find out if anyone here has seen it." Orion smiled at an old man that waved to him.

"Ah. Good idea Orion. Good idea." Oliver looked around. "Shall I ask here?"

"Oh, let's not. Let's get into the village so I might sit on a decent stool for a change." Lady Chantelle hadn't been oblivious to the conversation taking place behind her.

Alex squeezed Orion.

"Let's not go into the village, Lady Chantelle. Just the outskirts might be best."

"But if we go inside, there might be a tavern where we could get lunch."

"Have you the coin to feed us all?" Oliver's voice dripped sarcasm.

Lady Chantelle flushed and slowed the mare.

Oliver sped up to take the lead once more. "I thought not."

Orion sighed,

Alex jabbed him in the ribs. "I have coin in my pouch if you like."

"Not a good idea, Ally. Oliver will think you stole it."

"From where? We've been nowhere I could steal it from." Alex leaned to the side, trying to catch Orion's gaze.

The horse danced sideways, and Orion tightened the reins. "He'd think you took it from the castle--which you did--only he'd think you took what wasn't yours."

Sighing, Alex nodded into his shoulder. "It would be nice to eat a hot meal though. Those biscuits are apt to chip a tooth."

Orion laughed loud enough that Oliver and Lady Chantelle looked back, both with brows raised high.

Catching sight of a wayside trough up the road, Alex's stomach rumbled again. "Sir Oliver, I do think we could stop and eat lunch now. Perhaps there will be someone at the wayside you can ask about the dragon."

Alex's words had people on the fields staring again, and a couple put down their scythes and plows to meet them at the trough. While the horses drank, Alex dug through their pack, looking for the dried meat and even drier biscuits.

"Did I hear ye be looking for a dragon?" One of the men spoke to Oliver, glancing at his companion.

"Aye." Oliver turned from the drinking horses. "We've had word that a rampant beast has been attacking villages along the Paixor-Vreden border."

The man nodded, chewing on a piece of grass. "What ye looking for it to do."

"Defeat it of course." Oliver shook his head and turned back to his horse.

"Ye might want to talk to old Edith. She be here visiting her daughter since her village was destroyed, burnt to the ground I heard."

Oliver spun back to the men. "By a dragon? It was destroyed by a dragon?"

The man shrugged, looking to his companion before answering. "Not right sure. Ask old Edith."

"Where can I find old Edith?" Oliver was so excited at the possible lead, he was pulling his mount away from the tough, and the poor horse stretched its neck out, wriggling its lips trying to reach the water.

"Here, Oliver. Give me your reins." Orion grabbed the leads, easing them so the horse could drink.

"Is she close by?" Oliver didn't acknowledge Orion. Alex thought he might not even realize he no longer held the reins.

"Sure. Just up the road a bit. Cottage on the left, Can't miss it. There's a big pond full of ducks next to it."

Oliver pivoted back to them. Alex had just got her hands on the dried meat and was handing a piece to Lady Chantelle.

"Come on." He snatched the reins back from Orion, swinging himself back into the saddle. "We're wasting time."

"We're not wasting time, Oliver, we're eating." Orion took a piece of meat from Alex and put it in his mouth, He continued to let the remaining two horses drink.

"But-"

"Sir Oliver," there was s sharp edge to Lady Chantelle's tone, "we are going to eat first. I'm sure this old Edith will still be there in an hour."

"But-"

Orion sighed. "Oliver, have something to eat. Don't want you fainting from hunger when you finally get to ask this woman your questions."

"I won't faint." Oliver dismounted and took a piece of meat, chewing it loudly while his horse when back to the water trough.

Alex offered him a biscuit.

He grimaced, but accepted it. "We don't need to stuff ourselves though. Just eat enough to satisfy your hunger."

Rolling her eyes, causing both Lady Chantelle and Orion to giggle, Alex wondered how she could do more than just satisfy her hunger with the meager food they carried.

CHAPTER THIRTEEN

The cottage was just where the man had said it would be, a large pond sitting between it and the road, ducks and geese dotting its surface. A pig sty nestled next to a barn, and a larger pen housing a couple of cows and a small flock of sheep lay behind. A younger woman, a baby strapped to her back, was milking a goat.

Turning up the path toward the cottage, Orion lowed Oliver's horse. "Let me introduce us, eh?"

"What?" Oliver twisted in the saddle. "Why?"

Orion took a breath, but didn't answer.

"Because your people skills are sadly lacking. I'm sure Orion will be more successful at getting us a warm reception, and thus you'll get your questions answered." Lady Chantelle brought the mare up on the other side of Oliver.

Oliver snorted. "Best leave the boy here, then."

Alex sighed but dropped from behind Orion.

"Oliver, one day, you'll realize how wrong you've been." Orion spurred his horse forward, dismounting and bowing to the young woman with the baby.

"Why's he bowing to her?" Oliver's growl started in his gut and burst out his mouth.

Lady Chantelle sighed and shook her head. "Because he's got people skills, Sir Oliver. Highly developed people skills."

The young woman rose from her milking stool, accepted Orion's hand, looking off to the others and waving them forward.

"You stay here." Oliver spoke down to Alex, before snapping the reins and moving forward.

Shaking her head, Lady Chantelle stayed, fighting the mare a bit. The mare wanted to follow.

"Go ahead, Lady Chantelle. Sir Oliver may need your help, as well."

Lady Chantelle looked down. "He may need your help, too, you know. Even you have better people skills than he does."

Alex blinked at the backhanded comment, and when the mare started forward, with Lady Chantelle on her back, Alex followed on foot.

"Is old Edith here?" Sir Oliver had jumped right in.

"What do you want to know for?" The young woman stepped back.

"Sir Oliver." Lady Chantelle reprimanded. "Really. Help me get down before you worry the poor woman to death."

"What? But I need to know if the old woman is here." Oliver didn't bother helping Lady Chantelle.

"But you must do so politely."

Alex stepped forward, smiling at the young woman. "My apologies, miss. Sir Oliver is a bit anxious to verify a possible dragon attack."

"Dragon attack?" The young woman stopped her retreat, bouncing to calm the baby.

"Aye. An old man working the field up the road mentioned she was visiting because her village was destroyed by a dragon."

The young woman barked out a laugh, and the baby at her back let out a cry. the woman set on the stool, pulling the baby to her front to rock him in her arms. "She tells a good story about the attack."

"Was it a dragon?" Sir Oliver lunged forward, startling the young woman so that she almost toppled off the stool.

"Oliver." Orion grabbed his friend, retraining him. "You're being pushy again."

The woman stood up and pushed past. "She's in the house, napping. I'll go get her for you. She'll love having a new audience."

When the woman had disappeared inside the cottage, Orion smacked Oliver on the shoulder. "What did Lady Chantelle say?"

"What? Isn't that why we're here?"

"Well, yes, but there are nicer ways to act." Orion turned away and stoked the muzzle of his horse.

Oliver frowned, and stared at Alex. "I thought I told you to stay back?"

"Be glad she's here." Lady Chantelle was still atop the mare. "If she hadn't stepped in, the woman wouldn't be going to get the old woman for you now."

"Alex didn't do anything."

Lady Chantelle sighed. "Yes, she did. And I'm still waiting for you to help me down."

Sir Oliver grunted and looked to the cottage. There was no movement at the door, so he tramped to the mare and held out his arms. "Fine. Jump and I'll catch you."

"Jump?" Lady Chantelle raised her chin and stared off in the distance. "Ladies do not jump."

"Then how are you going to get down?"

"You are going to lift me down."

"What?" Oliver looked around, as if seeking assistance.

Alex ignored him, tending the mare, keeping her steady so that there wasn't an accident when Oliver finally figured out what he was going to do. Orion turned his back on his friend, winking at Alex. It seems he too wanted Oliver to help their companion.

"Well-" Oliver sputtered, waving his hands around, "here." He extended his hands to her, but did not touch her.

Lady Chantelle sniffed and sighed. "You are going to have to touch me. Put your hands at my waist, I will shift my leg over the horse, and then you can lower me to the ground."

"I can, eh?" Oliver clenched his hands to fists a moment, then stepped closer, placing timid fingers just above the trimmed line that demarked the waist of the red gown.

Bending into the hands, Lady Chantelle placed her hands on Oliver's shoulders and jerked her leg over the saddle. All might have gone well, but her skirt caught on a buckle and someone shouted from the cottage.

"Oy. You wot wants the dragon story?" And elderly woman stood on the stood, leaning heavy into the jamb.

Oliver jumped and turned, and Lady Chantelle dislodged her skirt, slipping down the side of the saddle into near nothingness.

"Oliver!" Alex' shout of warning made the young man spin back to the horse just in time to wrap his arms around Lady Chantelle.

Staggering, he stepped back, dragging the young woman with him. A ripping sound rent the air, and a long strip of white underskirt remained attached to the saddle, hanging limp down one side of the mare.

Alex held her snicker in, biting her lip to make it so. But Orion's shoulders shuddered with his silent laughter.

Oliver and Lady Chantelle were oblivious. Their faces flushed bright red, they stood next to the mare, arms wrapped around each other, Lady Chantelle's feet dangling half a foot above the ground.

"Well?"

Alex turned from the scene to focus on the woman. "Yes. We are the one interested in what happened with the dragon at your old village."

"Well, then, come in when yer done fooling around. I ain't gots all day ye know." With that, the woman turned and waddled back into the cottage.

Sir Oliver set Lady Chantelle on the ground, anxious hands smoothing over her skirts until he realized just what he was touching and froze, eye growing wide.

"That will be enough, Sir Oliver." Lady Chantelle's face grew even redder and her voice lilted high and faint. Straightening, she marched toward the cottage, head up and chin out, a small trail of white linen marking the dust behind her.

"Go on in, Oliver. Alex and I will just finish tying up the horses." Orion's voice cracked. Alex thought it might be from the strain of not laughing out loud.

Once Oliver was safely in the hut, Orion doubled over, gasping for air.

"He can likely still hear you." Alex tried to reprimand him, but thought some of the effect was lost when her own laughter--albeit softer--broke through her words.

Inside the air was smoky, the odor of cooking meat strong. The fire blazed in the grate, the sizzling roast set in a shallow pan, a kettle hung from a metal peg over the flames.

The old woman checked her meal and the kettle before settling in a rocker next to the fire. She nodded at the chairs by the table, and Sir Oliver held one out for Lady Chantelle before taking another for himself.

Orion looked at the last then looked to Alex, who nodded for him to sit. She stood just behind his chair, hands resting on the last slat, the door visible from the corner of her eye, just in case.

The woman rocked, the creak of wood against the stone hearth filling the space.

Sir Oliver cleared his throat; Lady Chantelle smacked his knee.

The old woman smiled and spoke. "It was three years ago now, I think. Maybe a little more. I lived with my son and 'is wife back then, at the foot of Roher Mountain. The village was called Miden, and sometimes Midland, but not often."

Oliver sighed and set back in the chair, crossing his arms.

Alex thought it funny he'd expected the story to be short.

"It was a winter dusk, the snow just startin' to drift down. The fires were lit and everything was being put in for the night. It came down from the mountain. I thought the 'owl was the wind from a storm." The woman blinked and stared into the fire. "No one thought it was a dragon."

"How do you know it was a dragon?" Orion asked, his voice cracking.

"I saw it. Came out of the 'ouse when I 'eard the screaming start. There it was, flying over the 'ouses, flames gushing from its mouth. Burned everything it touched it did."

"Did anyone fight back?"

"With what?" The old woman leaned forward in her chair, and ominous creak signaling it teetered on the edge of the hearth. "Ye can only fight fire with water, and it were all frozen."

"Surely there was some weapon-"

"No weapons. Most folks were 'erders, goat and sheep and a few cattle. No need fer weapons."

Sir Oliver nodded and took in a deep breath. "What color was this dragon?"

"White. Lie pearls."

"How could you tell the color?" Lady Chantelle stuck her nose up, glaring at Oliver.

"There were light from the moon, and from the fires it lit from that great maw. Not 'ard to tell."

"Were there any other survivors?" Orion asked his question in a low voice. Alex thought he didn't really want to know the answer.

"Not many. Me and another old woman. Our huts weren't close to the center, but on the outer bits, so we was able to git away. Couple others, but they went to live with family elsewhere."

"Why did you come here?" Alex felt the need to ask at least one question herself.

"Thought I'd be safe here. But now, there's dragon talk here too, and you coming with yer questions."

Alex nodded and stepped back from the chair. "We've taken enough of your time. Thank you for sharing."

"Wait. What?" Sir Oliver stood up. "But-"

Lady Chantelle rose as well, curtseying to the old woman. "Yes, thank you for your tale."

"Oliver," Orion addressed his friend, standing and stretching, "it is time to continue our journey."

The old woman clucked at them, pressing a biscuit into their palms before letting them leave.

"She might have been able to tell us more." Oliver hissed at Orion. He stood next to his mount, not bothering to untie it.

"She was already upset, Oliver. There was no sense making her tell us anything more. Her story was done."

"I don't believe it anyway." Lady Chantelle's announcement made Sir Oliver growl.

"You and your-"

"Oliver! Watch your tongue." Orion grabbed his friend's arm. "Let us be off. We can discuss the merits of the story later."

Oliver snorted, but took his horse's reins and took it's back. "There is nothing to discuss, Orion."

Orion sighed and helped Lady Chantelle gain the back of her horse. He shot Alex a look and she darted her eyes away. Oliver and Orion may have nothing to discuss, but she suspected Orion would be discussing it with her.

CHAPTER FOURTEEN

It was early morning. The sun was only just thinking of coming over the horizon. Alex sat near the remains of last evening's fire, and thought about breakfast. Lady Chantelle had been travelling with them for three days.

She was wearing on Alex's nerves. Nothing was done good enough for 'a lady', and Alex was getting tired of doing the all extra work for the extra person.

On top of that, Oliver's stash of food had moved beyond stale to inedible. Alex wasn't sure that she could stomach another dry biscuit, and they were now too far gone to moisten into a porridge.

Nodding, she decided to take care of breakfast herself this morning. They were camped not far from a village. She was not so out of practice that she couldn't procure something decent for them to eat.

Grinning, Alex rose from her seat and trotted in the direction of the faint footpath that crossed the meadow, moving away from her sleeping companions.

The village was already awake and thrumming with movement; the aroma of fresh-baked bread the village baker was preparing, the clink of the blacksmith starting work in the coolest part of the day. Children bustled, ferrying packages and animals from place to place. A baby cried through the open door of a cottage; the mother shushed it quickly, crooning so softly that Alex could not make out the words.

Alex missed this. She missed people. Oliver usually kept them away from villages and towns; Alex could only guess why. Perhaps it was to keep them from distractions? Or did he think it more likely they would find the dragon in the wild? Alex shrugged at her own thoughts, winding her way past the carts of fruits and vegetables.

In the end, heading back to the campsite, Alex had a still-warm loaf of bread, a fresh pot of butter, a bit of cooked bacon, and a sack of crisp apples. Her stomach rumbled, excited at the thought of the breakfast she would share back at camp.

Shivering a bit, she shook the coldness inside her away. It would not do for Orion to guess what she had done in the village, in her own way paying for the meager meal she had taken.

They were up, Oliver making the pot of black brew he needed so much, Orion tending the three horses and Lady Chantelle struggling to pack their blankets.

Oliver noticed her first. "I had hoped you wouldn't be coming back." He spat the words out without looking at her.

"Good morning to you, too."

Lady Chantelle smiled. "He's having trouble making his drink this morning. Orion wouldn't let him alone once he realized you were gone." She shook out a blanket she'd been trying to fold, trying again to match up the sides to make the neat squares.

"Where the....!" Orion noticed that she was back. "You could have...I thought you were..."

Alex grinned and held up her prizes. "I got breakfast."

Lady Chantelle stopped folding the blanket, dropping it back to the ground, eagerly stepping toward Alex, skirts in hand. "Breakfast? What did you get?"

Oliver snorted. "I'll eat none of that. 'Tis likely stolen from good folk that have done no one any harm." He sipped at his steaming cup, hissing as the drink burned his tongue.

Lady Chantelle snorted back. "Then I will enjoy your bit as well as my own. I am tired of stale biscuits and dried fruit." She sat down and looked expectantly at Alex.

Grinning, Alex offered her a bit of the bread and bacon then offered the pot of butter and a knife from her pack. She set the sack of apples on the ground.

"Mmmmm. Fresh bread. It has been so long since I have had fresh bread." Lady Chantelle closed her eyes and chewed.

Orion sat between them and held out his own hand for a share. He was shaking his head at Alex. "What did you do?" He took a bite of the bread without buttering it.

Alex busied herself with her own piece of bread, carefully buttering it. "I got us some breakfast."

"What did you *do*?" Orion leaned forward, trying to catch her gaze.

Oliver laughed. "He stole, Orion. He's a thief." He bit into one of his biscuits, grimacing at the taste in his mouth.

Orion sighed, ignoring Oliver. "Alex?"

Alex sighed, giving up so that Orion would stop asking. "The baker had a lame horse; I got the butter from him as well.

The woman with the bacon had injured herself, a bad cut on her hand. The apples I picked from a tree growing at the edge of an orchard." She still looked at her bread instead of at Orion.

"A woman?" Oliver spat coffee from his mouth.

Alex couldn't help but look up at his sharp tone. She pursed her lips. "She was old. She had fainted as the sight of the blood. She won't remember anything."

Oliver stood up, kicking spent ashes on the fire. "Stealing from an injured old woman. We ought to turn you in to them, you know."

"Oliver..." Orion's voice was soft.

"No! You let him..."

"You don't understand..." Orion stood as well, facing Oliver, his voice rising.

Lady Chantelle sat with her mouth open slightly, her buttered bread halfway to her mouth.

"I didn't hurt anyone!" Alex interrupted the fight. She hated when the two fought and she knew that Orion didn't like it either. She suspected that even Oliver, if pressed to make a decision, would say that he, too, disliked the arguments.

Lady Chantelle closed her mouth, the piece of bread dropping with her hand to her lap, no longer eating. Her head swiveled from Orion to Oliver and back.

Alex looked at each of them in turn then stooped to pick up the apples and her pack. Waiting only a moment, she turned and walked away.

"You need to apologize." Alex could hear Orion's voice chastising Oliver, their argument far from over.

"For what?"

"Alex is not a thief."

"Alex stole from the villagers!"

"And healed a horse and an old woman as payment!" This last was shouted. Alex heard the words, but kept walking. She did not dare turn around; she would not let Oliver see her tears.

"What are you talking about?" It was Lady Chantelle who asked the question, cutting into the argument with her soft voice.

"Alex can heal...wounds. It is...a gift." These words were spoken lower; Alex was almost too far away to hear them.

"Impossible!" Oliver was still shouting.

"You saw it Oliver, with your own eyes!"

"I saw nothing! It is impossible to heal wounds in such a manner. It was a trick, well played by your gypsy friend--but only a trick!"

Alex heard someone running behind her, but still did not turn around, even when that someone had caught up.

"Wouldn't it be better if you took your horse?" It was Orion.

Alex shrugged. "The three of you need it more than I do."

There was silence while they walked. They had reached the faint wagon track that led to the village.

"It's a long walk on foot."

"I have walked a longer distance."

A sigh. "Ally..." Orion stopped walking.

Alex continued, crossing the track, aiming for the tree line just ahead. It would be better to walk in the shade than under the heat of the sun.

"Alex!"

She stopped walking but did not turn around.

"We could tell them…"

Alex rounded on him, her words hissing in her hurt. "Why? Will he stop being nasty to me just because of who I am? Will she stop acting prissy and bossing me around because I am a princess?"

"She's not bossing you around. Not really. She just doesn't know any other way to act."

Alex continued, ignoring his words. "It shouldn't matter! It shouldn't matter what title I have or don't have!" Alex sobbed, swiping at a tear she hadn't know she'd shed. "I don't want them to like me, or respect me, because I am a princess. I want them to like and respect me because I am Alex, a gypsy. Because even a poor gypsy should have value."

Orion watched her, silent a moment, before speaking softly. "I want them to like you, too. I just don't think they are going to ever see past the peasant."

Alex swiped at another tear, then at her dripping nose.

"I need you to come with us. You know that, Alex. If I…" Orion swallowed hard; Alex could see his Adam's apple moving up and down. "The dragon…"

Alex squeezed her eyes shut, hard: the dragon.

They had to make Oliver realize that the dragon was likely not what he thought. Even Lady Chantelle, with her story, couldn't convince him. He was just too stubborn to admit when he was wrong.

Finding the old woman yesterday who had seen the dragon wreck her village had not helped their case.

"Alex, the dragon and its egg, they are going to need you. Lady Chantelle is on our side. We just have to work on Oliver a bit more." Orion put his hand on her shoulder, gently turning her back to the camp.

Still, Alex resisted, stiffening under his firm touch.

"Alex. Please. We don't have to tell them that you are a princess--in actual fact, the reigning ruler of Vreden. We just need to let them know that you are not the gypsy you appear to be." Orion kept his hand on her shoulder, gently pressing her back toward the others. "Please. You know I need you to stay with us. Soon, I will have to change. I can't do that if you leave."

Alex closed her eyes and took a deep, steadying breath.

She wanted to stay--she just didn't want to be royalty. She didn't like being royalty. She loved knowing who her parents are and being able to see them, though she hated that they were still trapped in the tapestry. She liked having food and shelter and a warm bed, and not having to worry about losing them. But, it annoyed her when people constantly bowed to her and agreed with everything she said--just because she was a princess. It frustrated her that other people couldn't accept how she was, but wanted her to be something else. Learn to curtsey, learn to dance, learn how to hold your head and how to hold your fork.

"Please." Orion spoke the word softly this time, whispering it almost directly into her ear.

Alex didn't dare open her eyes. She knew that Orion was close. She could smell the tang of his sweat, feel his heat brush against her skin. She thought that maybe the dragon was close to the surface. Alex knew that soon he would have to change; he would soon no longer have a choice.

"Okay." She nodded her agreement, keeping her eyes closed.

"Look at me."

Orion hadn't moved away. Alex took another deep breath and opened her eyes. Orion's face was close to hers, mere inches away. She stared into the intense blue of his eyes, seeing the fire in them that meant the dragon was close.

"Thank you." The words were barely audible. She felt them more than heard them, watching his mouth move to form them.

She nodded, starting when he bridged the space between them and placed a gentle kiss on her forehead. His lips lingered there, his breath stirring the wisps of hair that fringed her face.

Her breath rushed out of her lungs, and she stepped back, looking everywhere but at Orion. Butterflies danced in her stomach, their wings causing a tingling that touched her lungs, making it hard to take a full breath.

Orion's hand trailed down her arm to her hand, his fingers wrapping around hers, twining among them, tugging gently.

Allowing him to pull her along, she kept her eyes down, watching the ground and her toes. She wasn't sure if the others had been watching. She wasn't sure she could face them if they had been. Oliver already had ideas about her and Orion that would only be reinforced if he had seen that quick sign of affection.

Oliver and Lady Chantelle had not been watching; they had been packing up the camp. The blankets were folded and packed away--though the corner of one hung out of the lumpy-looking pack--and the fire had been doused and the horses saddled and made ready. Oliver scowled at their approach. "Why did you have to bring him back?"

"Alex needs to come with us."

"He does not need to come with us!" Oliver stood next to the sand-covered coals, fists planted on his hips.

"Yes, he does." Orion stared at Oliver, silently challenging him.

"No." Oliver walked to his horse, picking up the reins and placing one foot in a stirrup.

"Yes." Orion didn't move, but his free hand clenched into a fist, the other tightened its grip on Alex's hand.

Alex glanced at Lady Chantelle. She stood to one side, near Alex's horse, her head tilted to one side, watching Alex. Slowly, a faint smile appeared on her face, slowly growing in size until it was wide and caused dimples.

"Sir Oliver." Her voice was low, and caused Oliver to turn in her direction, dropping his left foot from the stirrup. "I don't think the "problem" you have with Alex is quite what you think it is."

Alex felt Orion stiffen even more beside her, his hand squeezing hers even harder.

Oliver sneered. "And what problem is that?"

Lady Chantelle turned to look at Oliver. "Alex is not a boy, but a girl."

Alex gasped, and tightened her own grip on Orion's hand. Oliver gaped, first at Lady Chantelle, then at Orion and Alex's joined hands; his mouth worked slowly, but no sound came out.

"I'm right, aren't I?" Lady Chantelle was still smiling.

Orion didn't answer. Alex, watching Lady Chantelle, nodded.

Lady Chantelle's grin turned into a laugh. "Oh, Sir Oliver! And you were so worried!"

"But..but..." Oliver was able to make sound come out of his mouth, but his hands were clenching and unclenching at his sides. "I know he's a girl. He...I mean, she...is still a peasant!"

"No." This time Orion spoke, his words crisp and short. "She is not a peasant."

Oliver said nothing, but waved his stiff arms at Alex, pointing to her pants and bright shirt.

Lady Chantelle smiled. "I had wondered about the dress you allowed me to wear. The quality was not something that a peasant would normally have. In many ways--like the stitching-- it was finer than my own. Even those," she pointed at Alex's trousers and shirt, "are of a fine quality, plain though they appear."

Sir Oliver gaped, his mouth hanging open, his hands frozen in their gesture towards Alex's attire.

Lady Chantelle laughed once again. "Sir Oliver, have you not heard my complaining about riding in a skirt? It is most difficult unless you have the proper saddle. I would say that Alex is simply wearing an outfit suitable to the task at hand."

Oliver snorted, turning back to his horse and mounting stiffly. He glared down at the others, his lips curling slightly. "It is unseemly for a lady to wear such garments."

Lady Chantelle straightened her back. "It is unseemly for a gentleman to refuse to admit when he is wrong."

Oliver huffed. "I do not believe that I am wrong."

Lady Chantelle shook her head, muttering something about "stubborn men" and approaching Alex's horse to mount. Taking the reins, she led the horse to a small boulder, standing on it to boost herself to the saddle.

Orion looked at Alex, relaxing slightly. "I guess you're riding with me again." He tugged at her hand, leading her to his horse. Taking the sack of apples, he tied it off to his saddle then boosted her to sit behind it. Mounting himself, he calmed the horse while Alex shifted to hold on to him, winding her arms around his middle.

"Let's go." Oliver didn't wait to see if the others followed his command before prodding his horse into a gallop.

CHAPTER FIFTEEN

"The dragon's lair is most likely back up river." Oliver's declaration stopped all activity in the camp.

"Why do you say that?" Lady Chantelle stood next to her fallen blanket, haphazardly trying to brush the tangled mess of her hair back from her face.

"That is the direction from which you came. We rescued you from here," he swept an arm around their small encampment and the river bend where they had indeed pulled the lady from the river.

They had traveled in a circle.

"That does not mean that I came from that direction with the dragon."

"We did not see you flying from down river." Oliver stood directly in front of Lady Chantelle, arms crossed over his chest.

"Perhaps we came from another direction and crossed over the river." Lady Chantelle raised her chin.

"If your story about the dragon is true, and I have nothing else to go on right now, I think the dragon was following the river. I think it not probable that you would have been lucky enough to fall from the dragon's back just as you flew over the river." Oliver looked rather smug.

Alex watched Lady Chantelle's face. It was obvious that she was trying to find something plausible to answer to Oliver's last declaration. It was also obvious that she could not find anything.

"I am not going back there."

"Then we will leave you here, alone." Oliver walked to his horse, petting it down and readying the saddle and bridle.

"You would leave a lady to fend for herself?"

Oliver turned from his mount, one hand still holding the bridle near the bit. "You were on your own before."

"I had no choice before. I was intent on escape only. I was not thinking of what to do after." Lady Chantelle twisted and pulled at her skirts.

"Then you best start thinking about that now. We will be leaving soon, up the river." Oliver pointed in the direction they would take then turned away, whistling quietly as he worked readying his horse.

Alex watched Oliver. She could not believe that he would leave Lady Chantelle to fend for herself, but she knew that he was intent on finding and destroying the dragon.

Orion squeezed her shoulder, nodding to the blankets. Alex began folding and packing, dousing the fire pit with water to ensure it was truly out.

Lady Chantelle paced, her hands continuing to worry the front of her dress. She was shaking her head and sniffing, occasionally swiping at a nest of hair that lodged in front of her eyes.

Alex packed the camp, shooting quick glances at Oliver and Orion who stood near the horses. They were talking quietly, their gestures harsh and sporadic. They were arguing. Again.

She sometimes wondered what their childhood friendship was like. Had they argued as much then as now?

"Are you ready?"

Oliver's words cut through Alex's thoughts. He was sitting on his horse, waiting.

Orion was leading his mount and hers.

Lady Chantelle was still pacing. "I cannot stay here alone. You must take me with you."

Oliver sat on his horse, regarding Lady Chantelle with narrowed eyes. "You will lead us to the dragon and its lair."

Lady Chantelle sighed. "There is no reason to go there. I have explained that the dragon is not the true threat."

"Of course the dragon is a threat! It is an evil beast and must be destroyed."

"She is not evil. I told you..."

Oliver cut across her words. "As you have said. But all dragons are evil. We must find its lair."

Lady Chantelle made to speak again, but Orion held up one hand, halting the conversation. "There is no use arguing with him. You do not want to stay here?"

Lady Chantelle shook her head, sniffing.

"Then we head up river."

She nodded.

Oliver grinned. "Let us mount up and get started then."

Alex walked to her horse and prepared to gain the saddle.

"What are you doing?" Oliver's smile disappeared and he frowned again.

"I am mounting my horse so that I may ride."

Oliver snorted. "That is a horse you stole. "tis not yours. Lady Chantelle may ride it."

Alex did not leave her horse, but stared at Oliver. "I am to walk?"

"'tis better for you to walk than the lady."

Alex had assumed that Lady Chantelle would sit behind one of the men this morning. She had not considered that it would be expected that one of them would walk.

Lady Chantelle approached the horse and Alex handed her the reins. "I shall need help. There is no rock."

"Oliver, help the lady." Orion's voice was a growl. He gained his own saddle and glared at his friend.

Oliver dismounted and assisted Lady Chantelle into the saddle. The lady sat on the horse, frowning. "You know this saddle is not made for a lady to ride."

Oliver sighed. "It is the only saddle we have. You were fine with it yesterday."

Lady Chantelle arranged her skirts and slipped to the side. Oliver caught her, pushing her back up.

"You will have to put your leg over the saddle." Oliver pushed her skirt up, preparing to help her with the adjustment.

Lady Chantelle squawked and slapped at his hands. "What are you doing?"

"I am assisting you to arrange yourself to ride. You will need to put your foot in the stirrup on the other side."

"But... but I am in a skirt." Lady Chantelle sputtered, her hands flapping in the air around her head.

"My lady," Oliver sighed, his voice low and controlled, "I promise that neither Orion nor I will dare to look at your ankles. Put your leg over and place your foot in the stirrup."

Alex didn't think Lady Chantelle was going to comply, but after a long, loud sniff and flip of matted hair, she slung her leg over the saddle to the other side and slipped her foot into the stirrup. A good deal of leg was on display, and even after she tugged on her skirt, one could view her ankles to her mid-calf. "I hope you realize that this is most inappropriate."

"Maybe you should have let Alex ride her horse." Orion hadn't moved yet, his horse standing still, chewing on its bit.

"And let the lady walk?" Oliver rounded on Orion.

"Lady Chantelle could have ridden with you."

Oliver sneered. "I will be in the lead. I cannot have my horse hampered by a second rider."

Orion said nothing. Lady Chantelle gathered the reins and waited to start. Oliver walked to his own horse and mounted. "Let's go." Oliver started and Lady Chantelle followed, bouncing in the saddle, though the mare only stepped to the side. The young woman kicked her heels and the mare started into a trot.

Alex sighed.

"Alex, come here." Orion held out his hand. Alex stared at it a moment, before raising her gaze to his face. He still wasn't happy. "Don't even think about walking. There is no reason to be stubborn. You couldn't keep up anyway."

"I am beginning to regret running away and coming with you." Alex walked to his hand and grasped it. Orion removed his foot from the stirrup and braced to pull her up. Alex placed her own foot in the stirrup and hopped twice for momentum before jumping to the horse's back. Settling behind Orion, she placed her arms around his middle.

"If you had not come, we would not have saved Lady Chantelle."

"You still would have saved her." Alex looked at Orion.

Orion half twisted in the saddle to look Alex in the eye. "You were looking for her, that is why you saw her. We would have lost her if you had not been here."

Alex thought for a moment, but did not voice her agreement.

He turned to the front, prodding his horse into a trot. "How did you know to look for her?"

Alex took a deep breath. "When I fell asleep on my horse, before I fell, I went to the meadow in my dream. Meredith showed me how to use magic to see into the future and I saw what was going to happen, before it happened."

She expected him to comment on her mention of the meadow or Meredith, but he did not.

"Don't worry about dozing while riding now. I won't let you fall."

"Okay." It was a whisper. Alex quirked a half smile at his back. "We'd best start catching up. I don't want to lose my horse completely."

Orion smiled back. "Hold on then."

Alex sat behind him, with her front pressed to his back, her arms wrapped around his middle. They easily caught up with Oliver and Lady Chantelle.

Lady Chantelle was having difficulty riding astride and wasted no time complaining about it. "This is most unseemly. Do not think I won't tell my father about this. He will know all you made me do."

"I've made you do nothing." Sir Oliver's voice drifted over his shoulder. He did not turn to back to face the young lady.

"Indeed you have. Not only have I had to ride astride, I've eaten the most horrible dry biscuits and been awakened by the horrendous stench of your morning brew."

Sir Oliver only grunted.

Orion changed the subject. "Perhaps if you explain in further detail what has happened, Oliver will begin to understand your dilemma better."

Lady Chantelle looked to Orion, her lips pressed tight together in disagreement or discomfort, Alex couldn't decipher which. "I do not think it wise. While the dragon is not evil, there is danger in that direction."

"So you have said!" Oliver spat the words at her, even turning his head to look at her. "You are no longer alone. Whoever this "lord" is, he will have to deal with us."

"True, but you will have to deal with his army. He claims to have the backing of King Rolando."

Alex raised her brows at this, and spoke up, leaning around Orion to see. "King Rolando is dead. The princess will not back this "lord" if he was backed by King Rolando."

"I do not know this. I would rather..."

"Yes, yes, yes!" Sir Oliver spat once again. He had fallen back to ride beside Lady Chantelle rather than in front of her. "We all know what you would rather do. If you are to remain with us and use that horse, you will have to head back up river." He shifted violently in his saddle, making his horse dance to the side.

"Please believe me, Lady Chantelle," Alex broke in softly, "King Rolando is dead. This "lord" has no backing from the royal family."

Lady Chantelle continued to look uneasy, her gaze darting from her three companions to the river upstream.

"If it makes you feel more secure," Orion added, "I was present when King Rolando died. He is well and truly dead. I also know that he attempted to kill Princess Alexandrina before he died. Anyone who was loyal to King Rolando will not be supported by her now."

Lady Chantelle stared at Orion a moment, before nodding her head. "I will continue up river with you, but I will not lead you to the dragon."

Oliver's nod was curt, and he spurred his horse off into a canter, muttering quietly, but not low enough for the rest of them not to hear. "Stubborn wench."

Lady Chantelle followed him, her horse shying under the reins. Orion, with Alex clinging to his back, brought up the rear.

"Why do you not lead?" Lady Chantelle asked over her shoulder.

"This is Oliver's quest; he is leader." Orion frowned at the question.

"You do not mind?"

"Not really. I do have to restrain myself from pulling rank, however, when we have a disagreement."

From the lead horse, Alex heard Oliver's snort. "He lies." Oliver raised his voice to ensure all could hear. "He does not bother to restrain himself at all!"

Orion laughed, the sound mingling with the soft chuckles of Oliver.

Alex smiled. It was pleasant when Orion and Oliver were not fighting. Oliver was on the trail of the dragon once again, and so he was happy.

Lady Chantelle looked confused, her gaze darting from Orion to Oliver and back. Craning her head around Orion's broad shoulders, Alex grinned at her. "They are friends from childhood. You will find that they do not often act like prince and subject."

"Nor do you."

Alex shook her head in agreement. "No, I do not." And ducked her head back around before she completely unbalanced herself. Taking a breath, she leaned into Orion's back, pressing her cheek between his shoulder blades, and relaxed.

CHAPTER SIXTEEN

The rocking of the horse's steps put Alex to sleep. Orion was a warm presence, and she felt safe.

She did not visit the usual meadow, where Meredith's tent was set, but the small glade where she met Orion when he was still a dragon. The leaves filtered the sunlight, though they were dense enough she could not see the sky. Birds chirped and squirrels chattered.

Alex looked down. She wore a gown and her hair was long, the ringlets reaching to her waist. Wriggling her toes, she felt the soft butter of the leather slippers on her feet.

In this dream-glade, she was a princess.

Following a faint path in the grass, Alex stumbled upon a small cottage, not unlike the one Old Bertram had lived in at the foot of the Eastern Mountains. Its walls were brick and the roof thatched. Chickens squawked in a pen, pecking at the ground for their dinner.

"Hello?" Alex didn't recall seeing the cottage before. Of course, when she'd visited the glen before, she'd been focused on Orion and his story. They hadn't explored at all.

Alex rapped on the door, but there was no answer. Pushing, the door opened without a sound. The chickens kept up their noise and foraging, undisturbed that someone new was in their midst.

The interior was dim, but faint light seeped in through simple linen curtains. There was a table and two chairs, a hearth with firewood stacked but unlit, a locked cabinet and a smaller door.

"Hello?" Alex called out once more. She didn't want to trespass, but she was curious about this house in her dream. Though she would like to believe no one would harm her in her dreams, she didn't trust Meredith, and was unsure that she could trust anyone here, either.

There was still no answer, so Alex moved the curtains aside and let more light in. The large hasp on the cabinet looked heavy enough to topple the smallish piece of furniture. It looked delicate, with scrolls and filigree etched into its surface.

Alex pulled on the lock, but it held. Surely if this were her dream, she could open it?

Since it held fast, Alex moved on to the small door, and found that it opened easily. She expected it to be a bedroom, or perhaps a cooling larder, but it was not. It was a library.

The room's walls were covered in shelves, and the shelved sagged under the weight of the book they held. A writing desk stood in the center, a tall stool set beside it.

Alex ran her fingers over the books, and a thrill of magic swept up her arm. These books were special.

the chickens outside shrieked, making Alex jump. Listening, she left the room, closing the door behind her.

"Hello?" The extra light in the main room meant Alex could see everything there. Out the window, the chickens flapped, hovering just above the ground, trying to fly away.

Fear knotted in Alex's stomach. She had no weapon. how could she protect herself from whatever danger the birds sensed?

The cry of a hawk echoed through the hut, and Alex ran to the door, stepping out and looking up. The raptor flew above the leaves, casting a dark, flitting shadow over the ground. It cried again, stuck above the canopy.

Panicked, the chickens raced for cover, their wings flapping and kicking up dust.

Taking pity on the creatures, Alex jogged forward to open the door to the coop, and the birds rushed the door, squawking and scrambling to get inside.

the hawk called again, and its cutting shadow sliced the glade once more. Clouds gathered, dimming the sun and a cool breeze danced through the leaves. Shivering, Alex wished she had a cloak, and there one was, green and long and draped over the lower limb of a large oak.

Taking the cloak, Alex threw it over her shoulders, relishing the instant warmth. The breeze grew colder, until even the cloak could not stop her shivers. Snowflakes drifted down, settling on leaves and grass. The cold sparkle looked at odds with the lush summer green of the glen, and Alex knew it was wrong.

Something bad was doing this. Something evil.

But what?

Teeth chattering and toes frozen where she walked through the gathering snow, Alex traced her way back to where she'd arrived. The sheltered glade was frozen, a stark grey sky peeking between the barren twigs of the trees.

"I need to go back." Alex spoke aloud, though to who she didn't know. She had come here on purpose, had thought about it when she'd fallen asleep leaning against Orion.

So how could she go back?

The opening in the wood that led to the meadow was just ahead to her left. Could she go that way? Could --would -- Meredith help her?

Alex's stomach clenched. No. She suspected that Meredith would be upset that she had come here and not to their meadow. Glancing around at the ever-frostier world, Alex wondered about the glade. It had once been lush and green, and was now in the midst of winter. Was it too affected by whatever was doing this?

Her magic was cold. Was her magic doing this?

Whipping around, Alex ran back toward the cottage. Maybe she could start a fire? Maybe she had to warm herself up.

A jutting root tripped her and she sprawled to the ground, the cold from the snow creeping into her gown, her cloak--her skin. Shivering, she struggled to her feet, but fell back to the ground. Something had snagged her dress, and it was caught. Tugging, she tried to free it, but could not.

"Orion!" Alex did not know why she called for her friend. But he had been here before. Perhaps he could come again, and help her.

The hawk called again, closer, and dipped below the leaves, through the opening in the glade. Wings pumping, it rushed at Alex, claws outstretched.

Alex screamed and fainted.

"Ouch!" Orion twisted in the saddle, grappling at Alex's arms.

Gasping, Alex opened her eyes, choking, writhing where she straddled the horse.

"Easy, Alex, or you'll fall off--again." Orion grabbed her, steadying her with his arms while he slowed the horse with his knees. "It's okay, you're right here with me."

"The meadow!"

"What meadow?" Orion glanced ahead at their companions, but neither seemed to have noticed their conversation and lagging progress.

"The dream meadow. The one you visited me in. It's freezing over." Alex tried to keep her voice steady. "Something is wrong."

"You went there? In your dream, like before?"

Alex nodded. "It's getting easier. But something's wrong. I think my magic is destroying it."

"Why do you say that?" Orion pulled his mount to a stop, turning in the saddle enough that he could face her.

"It's snowing there. And it was summer when I arrived."

Orion watched her, a frown marring his face. "So why do you think it is your magic at fault?"

"My magic is like ice, Orion. It tries to freeze me. What if it is freezing the meadow?"

"Okay. So maybe your magic is the problem." Orion tucked a stray curl behind her ear, his fingers like a flame against her cheek, then cupped her jaw, leaning close. "Or whatever is attacking your dream meadow is also attacking your magic."

CHAPTER SEVENTEEN

It was a long way back up river. Lady Chantelle rode silent for the most part. She sat stiff in the saddle, her body rocking against the rhythm of the mare, and she kept fussing with her skirts when they exposed too much leg.

Alex was also uncomfortable; she continued to ride behind Orion, her arms wrapped around his lean torso, her cheek pressed against his back. She was uncomfortable, yes, but found herself happy that it was she riding behind him, and not Lady Chantelle.

She busied herself with thinking about what Orion had said about her magic? Could he be right? Was something attacking her magic? It didn't seem possible to her, but then, having magic had seemed impossible at one point in her life.

All the thinking was making her head ache, and she stopped chasing the possibilities in her mind. She was afraid to sleep though, so she focused on their surroundings: the trees, the rocks, the birds overhead.

Orion also remained quiet, though he was alert, looking around them constantly. He shivered sometimes, and Alex wondered if it was the dragon inside making itself known, or if he sensed something else. She became more alert, keeping her own careful watch.

Oliver was not quiet. He asked Lady Chantelle questions--questions that she rarely answered--but it did not stop him from posing another, and another. Alex thought that perhaps he would begin shouting at her again, but he never did.

That evening, when they made camp, they ate the last of the apples and bread, and briefly discussed obtaining additional sustenance.

"I can visit another village." Alex offered. She was shaking out the blankets and arranging them around the fire.

Oliver sneered. "We do not need any more stolen goods."

"Oliver," Orion's voice was clipped, "I explained before that Alex did not steal the food. He traded for it."

"He had nothing to offer in trade."

Lady Chantelle watched the two young men, her lips a thin, tight line in her face. "Why do you still call Alex "he" when we all now know that she is not?"

Alex paused with one blanket dangling in the air.

Orion answered. "It is best that anyone who meets us think Alex is a boy. It is easiest if we always say "he.""

Oliver sneered again. "Alex is likely a thief running from the law. The white mare was likely stolen and that is why he is running now."

"Sir Oliver, you do not remember the courtyard? That Baron Castellan was there, explaining that I was to accompany you, as a court observer of sorts? The mare was ready and waiting for me to ride her. It was certainly not stolen." Alex watched the blanket in front of her.

Lady Chantelle considered Oliver, then turned to Alex. "This dress," she indicated the one she was wearing, the one that Alex had provided when they first met, "is it stolen?"

Alex did not answer, instead violently flipping the blanket in the air and placing it on the ground, folding it once down its length.

"Why would a gypsy own such a dress?" Oliver spat the words out.

Orion stood up, his hands balled into fists at his sides. "That is enough, Oliver. You know nothing of Alex's story, so you have no right to pass judgment. I have told you that he is not truly a gypsy, and that it is a disguise."

Oliver stood as well, facing Orion over the spurting flames of the campfire. "That is right. I do not know Alex's story and I think I have a right to know it. For all I know, we are being hunted by lawmen right now. And we will be thrown in prison along with your gypsy."

Orion took a deep breath. Alex could see his chest expand and hear the whoosh of air he expelled. "Princess Alexandrina would not let that happen."

"How do you know?" Oliver shouted now, waving his hands about his head.

Alex winced; he was loud and angry, spitting his words at Orion.

"I know Princess Alexandrina."

Lady Chantelle gasped. "You were introduced to her?"

Orion looked to Lady Chantelle. "I sponsored Oliver's visit so he could make his request to her."

"I know you said that King Rolando was dead, but I did not know you were that close to the princess."

Oliver sneered once more. "You are close to a lot of people in Vreden, aren't you?"

Orion snorted and Alex caught sight of his brief smile. "Not as many as you think."

"Can you sponsor a meeting for me with the princess? So that I could ask for her help?" Lady Chantelle tugged on Orion's sleeve.

"Of course. I am sure that Princess Alexandrina will help you."

Lady Chantelle smiled. "Can we go to her now?"

"No!" Oliver was back to shouting. "We are looking for the dragon!"

Lady Chantelle rounded on Oliver, jabbing her finger at him. "You are looking for the dragon. In case it has passed your notice, none of us think you should be looking for it. We all think you should just give up and let it be. If you want to go looking for something evil to vanquish, try finding the man that kidnapped and imprisoned me."

Oliver spat on the ground and strode off toward the forest.

Alex sat on the blanket; Lady Chantelle sat on the saddle she was using for a stool. Orion continued standing, staring at the spot where Oliver had disappeared. Alex could see the ripple under his skin, the slight glint of scale.

Orion needed to transform.

"I am also going for a walk." Orion turned to stride away, heading the opposite direction from Oliver.

Lady Chantelle rose from her perch. "But, Orion..."

Alex gently took her arm, pulling her back down to the saddle. "Let him go. All will be well. Let them get rid of their anger."

"But we are left alone."

Smiling, Alex patted the side of her boot. "I have my dagger. We are as safe as we are with them around."

Alex had often been left alone with the wagon and Murray, the old donkey that pulled it for Gwennie. It had been necessary, sometimes, when Gwennie needed to negotiate for permission for Alex to perform her magik show, or to gain permission to cross someone's land.

"Don't worry, Lady Chantelle. There is nothing to be afraid of. I doubt that either of them are truly that far away, and will come if we call out."

Lady Chantelle nodded, but still looked apprehensive.

"Why don't we finish getting things ready for the night while they are away? It will give us something to keep our minds off the fact that they are gone."

Alex showed Lady Chantelle how to shake out the blankets, and fold them for sleeping, so that half could be under and half over the person using it.

"Why did you shake the blankets out first?" Lady Chantelle stood back from Alex, her hands clasped in front of her.

Alex smiled. "To get the bugs out."

Lady Chantelle's eyes grew wide, and she nodded. "I will make sure to shake the blankets out, as well."

When Alex took the last of the food supply in a sack and hoisted it up a tree, Lady Chantelle followed, a slight frown marring her features.

"Why do you put the food so far away from us?"

Alex grunted, pulling on the rope the sack was tied to. "To keep the animals that might find it interesting a good distance away. They may take the food, but will likely leave us alone."

Lady Chantelle followed Alex every step she took, continually asking questions. She reminded Alex a bit of Oliver; once he got going, he didn't stop either.

"Why did you place the firewood that far from the fire? Would it not be better to keep it closer, so that we can easily reach it to keep the fire going?"

"Yes, it would be easier, but it might also catch fire when we do not want it to."

Lady Chantelle sat next to the fire, arranging her skirts. "Why did you dig a hole for the fire?"

"The pit will help keep the fire contained. I dug down to the dirt, away from the roots, so that the fire cannot smolder there and travel out from the pit, causing a larger fire that could destroy the forest. The dirt from the hole will be used to smother and cover the fire in the morning."

Lady Chantelle nodded. "I remember seeing Sir Oliver use dirt to put the fire out, but I did not realize, or even think to wonder, where it came from."

She stopped asking questions. "I do not know much to help you."

Alex cocked her head, pondering this new, uncertain Lady Chantelle. "You do now."

Lady Chantelle looked up from the fire and smiled at Alex. It was a small smile, but Alex was happy to see it. They were silent for several minutes when Alex decided to start asking questions.

"What is it like living in a grand manor with servants?"

Lady Chantelle shrugged her shoulders. "It is nice, because anything you want is brought to you. But it is sometimes difficult to find a place to be alone. Sometimes, I wanted to find a cupboard and hide inside it. Other times, it was difficult because I had no one to talk to; all the other women were busy with their work."

Alex smiled. "Did you ever hide in a cupboard?"

"No. Papa would worry too much, and I dare not make Papa worry."

"What did you do in the winter? We usually--that would be me and Gwennie, the gypsy woman who took me in--we usually found a place that let us stay for the winter months, and did odd jobs to earn our keep."

Lady Chantelle stared at Alex. "I usually spent the winter sitting next to the fire, tatting or crocheting while Papa and his steward went over the manor's finances and planned next year's crops."

"What did you do in the summer?"

"I would sit in the upper bailey, tatting or crocheting, and watch Papa train with his men. Or wait for him to come home from checking the crops and livestock."

"Did you never cook?"

Lady Chantelle shook her head, her unkempt tresses whipping the air, and Alex winced as a ball of matted hair bounced against the girl's forehead. "Goodness, no! Papa would have had a fit if he'd ever found me in the kitchens. 'tis certainly not the place for a lady."

Alex picked up a stick and poked at the fire, sending sparks into the air. "Did you ever ride?"

Lady Chantelle nodded. "Sometimes, when Papa could go with me. We would ride through the villages, and I would watch Papa speak to the people and check over the holdings."

Alex wondered if she would have to learn to tat and crochet now that she was going to be queen. She hoped not.

"What did you do in the summer?" Lady Chantelle stood to fetch another piece of wood and place it in the fire.

Alex smiled, remembering. "I did magic tricks." The memories made her homesick, and she found herself missing Murray and the tiny wagon.

Lady Chantelle stared at her.

"I would dress as a boy – pretty much like I am now – only in bright colored clothes, and perform magic acts at festivals. Folks would give us coin for entertaining them."

"Did you like it?"

Alex thought a moment and smiled. "Yes. Most of the time."

The two were silent, each staring into the crackling fire. The heat from the flames kept the chilly air at bay, though Lady Chantelle rubbed her hands over her arms.

"Do you believe in real magic?"

Startled by the question, Alex turned to look at Lady Chantelle. The young lady stared into the flames, the flickering tongues reflecting in the perfect green of her eyes and lending a reddish hue to her blonde hair.

Alex wasn't sure how to answer. "Real magic?"

Lady Chantelle sighed, leaning back from the fire and looking up into the sky. "You will think me silly, I suppose. But, I believe in real magic. Not the tricks of magicians--though that is fun to watch--but the kind that can be dangerous."

"Why do you think magic is real?"

"Because I have seen it." Lady Chantelle brought her gaze to Alex's face, the shimmer of tears filling them. "The lord that imprisoned me used magic to control the dragon."

"What kind of magic?"

Lady Chantelle stared back into the flames, rubbing her arms again. "He wore a necklace--an amulet I suppose it should be called. It glowed when he used it. And when he used it, the dragon did whatever he told it to do. He used it to force the dragon to give him her egg."

Alex stiffened. An amulet? That glowed when it was used? She thought of the separated ruby and sapphire and broken golden chain that rested in the top of her trunk at Vreden Castle.

"Yes, Lady Chantelle. I believe in real magic, too."

They were still sitting by the fire, in comfortable silence, when Oliver returned.

"Where is Orion?"

"He went for a walk." Lady Chantelle leaned closer to the fire.

"He left you here alone?"

"Alex was with me."

Oliver snorted and glared at Alex. Alex sighed, standing and stretching. "He needed to lose his anger as much as you did."

"I did not lose my anger."

"I can tell." Alex moved to her blanket and crawled under. "Good night." She closed her eyes, trying to ignore Oliver's stomping and cursing as he readied for sleep.

"Goodnight, Alex." Lady Chantelle's voice was soft and close. Alex opened her eyes to find that Lady Chantelle had moved her blanket closer to Alex's.

Alex smiled at her and went to sleep.

CHAPTER EIGHTEEN

Alex found herself in the dream meadow, the sun shining down on the top of her head, a soft breeze ruffling her curls. Taking a deep breath, Alex smiled and turned, catching sight of the tall pines, the blue sky and the puffy white clouds.

The camp sat at the far end, near the forest, as far away from the misty wood as possible. Meredith sat on one of the stools, hands folded in her lap, watching Alex.

Alex approached, not letting the constant glare intimidate her. "Good day, Meredith."

Meredith did not respond.

Alex shrugged and walked the perimeter of the meadow, glancing occasionally at Meredith, who remained sitting, stiff as one of the pines, on her stool. She found the one path that led through the misty wood, and another that she knew not where it led. She was pondering following it when the entire meadow turned to mist in front of her eyes.

She heard the cry of a hawk. It was loud, like the raptor was right at her ear.

The mist blinded her, and she could see nothing. Though the sound of the hawk's cries were loud, other sounds were muted, like they were far away.

The hawk's cry changed into a screech of pain, the cry cutting of in an instant.

Standing, surrounded by cooling fog, Alex tried to see where she was. She thought she might still be in the dream meadow, but she wasn't certain. It felt like ground beneath her feet, but she couldn't see it.

Stretching one hand down and squatting, she searched with her fingers, finding stiff grass and dirt. She dug her fingers into the soil; it was dry and hard, and small stones bit into her skin.

"Alex!" Meredith called.

Alex opened her mouth to respond, but stopped before voicing her reply. Did she want Meredith to help her? Where had the mist come from? Was it there to hinder her journey to the meadow? Or help her in some way?

Though the mist was cool against her skin, she did not feel threatened. It did not press in against her, to clog her lungs, but drifted about, like an airy blanket.

Alex stood, taking soil in her fist, and stepped back one step, and again. She walked backward, away from Meredith, whose calls grew fainter until they faded away.

Stopping, Alex listened. She could not hear the hawk either, though if the cry of pain was true, she suspected the bird was dead, or at least maimed.

She squinted into the fog, and saw shapes. Trees. Pines. She stepped ahead, hand outstretched, and felt the trunks, the battered bark, the still moist needles. Breaking one off, the scent reached into her lungs, dragging her away from the meadow.

She was in the forest, the gnarled oaks growing dense, packed together, twisting and turning amongst themselves, folding in on each other so that it was hard to discern one tree from another. The path at her feet was ragged and lined with scrawny ferns and bracken.

Taking a breath, Alex straightened and moved down the path, placing one step firm against the earth before taking another. She had been here before, following a red string to Orion and safety. And though there was no string this time, she knew where she was going, and was not afraid.

The glade was still frozen, though it had stopped snowing. Icicles hung from the branches, some reaching to meet the snow and ice below. The sliver of sky loomed grey and heavy.

Alex still wore her trousers and heavy jacket. Her hair remained short and tied back. She remained Alex.

Was it a sign? And was it good or bad.

She continued forward to the cottage, opening the door without bothering to call out. She knew no one would answer. The coop was silent. She didn't dare check on the chickens, afraid at what she would find.

Inside, the curtain was still pulled away from the window, letting the weak winter sunlight flood the room. She tried the cabinet: it was still locked. She moved to the door, and it opened, a spine shivering shriek accompanying the movement.

Alex left the door open, turning to the fireplace. The wood still waited, stacked like a cone, kindling bundled beneath the larger blocks. Standing before it, Alex held out a hand, thinking "fire."

Nothing happened.

She looked about the mantle for a striking stone, but there was nothing. How could she start the fire? If she could start it, would the whole glade warm up?

It didn't make sense that it would, but then the meadow and glen didn't make sense anyway.

Alex entered the small room, once more running her fingers over the spines of the books. Stopping, she listened, waiting for the screech of predator from above.

There was nothing but silence.

She pulled a book from the shelf, running her palm over the leather cover. Before, there had been a tingle of warmth, but now there was nothing. Had the cold seeped away the warm magic of the books? Is that why the snow had come?

Replacing the book, Alex wandered the room, checking the drawers of the desk, checking the lamp for a tinderbox. She opened a stray book or two, but the light was too dim to read what was there. Taking it to the other room, she found the words to be in a language she couldn't understand.

Giving up, Alex left the book on the table, the door to the room open, and left the cottage. There was no sense in staying if there was nothing to be done there.

CHAPTER NINETEEN

Alex was the first to awaken in the morning, shivering in the mist that had sunk to the ground. It was not just that the mist was cold, but for a moment, she wondered if she was still in the meadow, stuck and lost.

The fire had burnt out in the night and Oliver lay, snores rumbling from his chest, on the other side, showing his back to them. Lady Chantelle lay silent, her hands once again clasped beneath her cheek.

Sitting up, Alex saw Orion, sleeping on his back, one arm stretched out toward the fire. He looked relaxed. But then, Alex thought, he was asleep; he *should* looked relaxed when asleep.

He shifted, his auburn hair falling over his forehead, and again Alex fought the urge to brush it aside. He pulled his arm in to his side and opened his eyes, smiling when he saw her sitting up and awake.

"Feeling better?" Alex spoke first, her voice husky from the morning.

"Much." Orion sat up as well, stretching his arms over his head.

Alex ducked her head and busied herself with her blankets to stop herself from watching him move. His muscles were lean, and he moved with sinewy strength. Observing him made her insides quiver and she wanted to touch him, to feel those muscles just beneath his skin.

Clearing her throat, Alex stood and began prepping the fire and breakfast.

Orion watched her, his eyes at half mast, chin in his palm, elbow on a raised knee. Shaking his head, he rose and went to fetch water.

Between the two of them, they had their blankets away, the fire restarted and breakfast begun, including the water for tea and Oliver's black morning brew, when Lady Chantelle and Oliver awoke.

Oliver sat grumping next to the fire, waiting for his drink. Lady Chantelle busied herself with shaking out the last two blankets and folding them to stow them away.

Orion watched her, glancing once at Alex, eyebrow raised.

Alex smiled and shrugged.

Shaking his head, smiling, Orion went to check on the horses.

Oliver grunted, sipping at a mug of what he called coffee. Lady Chantelle stooped over the fire, carefully stirring the pot of eggs Orion had scavenged from the forest earlier.

Oliver frowned at her. "What are you doing?"

Lady Chantelle looked up, pushing the matt of her hair back from her face. "I am helping with breakfast."

"Let Alex do it."

"Alex is busy." Lady Chantelle nodded at Alex, who was carefully packing their bags and food stores. "I am perfectly capable of stirring the eggs."

Oliver continued frowning. "It is not your place to stir the eggs. Have Alex do it."

"I am eating am I not?"

Oliver paused a moment, his mug half way to his mouth, the steam spiraling up past his face. "Yes."

"Then I can help with cooking the food."

"You do not know how."

"I am learning how."

"You should not have to."

"Perhaps not, but as it is best if we all pull our own weight, I am learning to do the cooking."

Alex returned, checking the scrambled eggs. "How are they doing?"

"They are no longer runny."

"Then they should be done. Dish them out onto the biscuits. Their steam will help to soften them."

Lady Chantelle grinned at Alex and dished out the breakfast.

"What do you think you are doing?" Oliver stood up, his now empty mug hanging from his fingers.

Alex smiled sweetly. "I am doing as milady asked, and showing her how to cook."

Oliver narrowed his eyes at her, snorted, and walked to join Orion with the horses.

"He does not like you?"

"No."

"Do you know why? I cannot figure it out." Lady Chantelle stood, stick in hand, watched their male companions.

Alex sighed, looking to where Oliver and Orion stood. "I think he wanted this to be a two-man only quest. I was rather foisted upon him."

Lady Chantelle smiled, carefully ladling steamy eggs onto an open biscuit. "Orion likes that you are here."

Alex grinned. "Orion and I are friends."

Lady Chantelle frowned, setting the full plate on the ground. "Oliver and Orion are friends?"

"Yes. They shared a school room as boys."

"Did you know Orion then?"

"No, I met Orion later."

"Ahh."

Alex looked up at Lady Chantelle. "What?"

"Perhaps, Oliver is thinking that he is in competition with you for Orion's friendship."

Alex stared at Lady Chantelle. "No, I don't think that is it. He did not want me to come, and was quite vehement about it before he knew that Orion and I were friends."

"Oh."

"He does not think highly of me as I am a gypsy." Alex rolled her eyes.

Lady Chantelle snorted, almost dropping a scoop of eggs on the ground. "You speak quite well for a gypsy."

Alex cocked her head. "I am in disguise, remember?"

"Yes. And I knew that before you told me, or suspected anyway. And not just that you are a girl dressed as a boy. It is obvious from the way you speak and act that you are not a gypsy."

"Oh?"

"I doubt that Oliver notices such things."

"Orion noticed. When we first met."

"Orion notices many things, I think."

A twig crackling behind made both girls spin around. Oliver and Orion approached, talking quietly to each other. Orion was shaking his head, looking like he was trying not to laugh. Oliver was waving his hands and looked quite agitated, his cheeks flushed a deep red.

Alex glanced at Lady Chantelle and whispered. "I don't think Oliver likes that you are cooking.

"He gave me that impression, as well." Lady Chantelle stuck her chin high, narrowing her eyes to watch the two young men march closer.

"Lady Chantelle," Orion was unable to keep the laughter from his voice, "how dare you try to cook!"

Lady Chantelle arched her brows. "There is no reason for me not to. I have nothing else to do in the mornings and Alex has many chores."

"That is not the point..." Oliver began, but was unable to finish the sentence.

"That is exactly the point." Lady Chantelle stood up, fisting her hands by her sides. "I can help by doing some of the chores. Cooking breakfast is one of the easier tasks."

"Very well." Orion clapped his hands together. "You may perform the cooking from now on. Is breakfast ready?"

Lady Chantelle beamed and handed Orion one of the plates. She then held one out to Oliver, who looked at the plate but did not take it. Lady Chantelle handed it to Alex instead, who accepted it with a smile.

"Thank you, Lady Chantelle."

"You are most welcome." Lady Chantelle sat down with her own plate, taking up her fork to stab into the egg and biscuit.

"It is unseemly."

"It is unseemly for me to even be here, Sir Oliver. There is no sense in pretending otherwise. It is best that I begin to help. I only wish I had realized it earlier."

Oliver took a deep breath, his chest puffing out in front of him, and made to continue speaking.

But, Orion cut him off. "Oliver, once we are back at the Summer Castle, I am sure no one will take offense to Lady Chantelle having helped with the chores on this quest."

Oliver dropped down hard beside Orion. "It is just, I would hate for the Princess Alexandrina to think ill of Lady Chantelle. The princess seemed so...so..."

"Out of place?" Alex offered.

Oliver turned purple. "How dare you speak thusly of your ruler! You are lucky you still have your tongue."

Alex raised her brows. "I meant no disrespect by the comment."

"Oliver, relax. There is no one here to take offense by what we say. Trust me, I do not think the princess will cut out Alex's tongue for it." Tongue stuck to his cheek, Orion looked like he was going to burst from laughter.

"One can never be too sure of that. A good and just ruler can turn in an instant." Oliver stared at Alex, his eyes boring into her. "You must remember to be careful at all times. You cannot truly trust anyone with your true opinions."

Alex could not believe that Sir Oliver was concerned for her, but it was Orion who spoke.

"Who turned, Oliver?"

"It is of no consequence now."

"Oliver, please tell us." Lady Chantelle put her plate down and placed one hand on his arm.

Oliver sighed. "There was a visiting royal family, after Orion went missing. They came to pay their respects to your father, King Mychal." Oliver looked at Orion, who nodded in understanding: it had been a political move. "The son, I thought he was a friend. That he was treating me the same as you had done. I confided in him that I suspected there was more to your disappearance than what anyone thought."

Oliver paused, his head bowed. He dug the toe of his boot through the closest bit of ash. "He told one of the guards, and my father was investigated as playing a role in what happened. He was almost put to death, until your mother convinced your father to speak to me in person, and I explained what I had said."

Oliver looked to Orion. The young man shook, the tremors noticeable even in his body. "My father almost died because of a casual comment I made to someone I thought was a friend."

"Sir Oliver," Alex licked her lips; they were unexpectedly dry, "you have no need to fear Princess Alexandrina. She would never do such a thing.'

"You cannot know this. Not even Orion can know this."

Alex pursed her lips and took a breath, looking away from Oliver and Lady Chantelle. She caught Orion's gaze; he was staring at her intently. Alex shook her head at him and stood up, placing her breakfast on the ground. "I am going for a walk. I am no longer hungry."

She could feel Orion's eyes on her back, and hear the low murmur of Lady Chantelle speaking, but she did not look back.

Alone, the trees providing shade and cover, Alex sat, covering her eyes with her hands to stem the tears that threatened to leak out. She couldn't just tell Sir Oliver and Lady Chantelle who she really was. It would ruin everything.

And maybe she wasn't Princess Alexandrina, anyway. She hated that life, much preferred this one, travelling and free.

Orion thought it would solve everything if she just told them. He didn't understand. If he wanted her to tell her secret so badly, why didn't he tell them his?

CHAPTER TWENTY

It was late in the morning when they started out, far later than Oliver wanted, and he was not pleased, though he said nothing about it. Alex took her horse and mounted before anyone could mention who was riding with whom.

Orion said nothing, helping Lady Chantelle to gain the back of his horse, then pulling himself up to sit in front. He glared at Alex though.

Oliver frowned.

Alex ignored all of them, spurring her horse to the north and taking the lead. She was surprised when they followed, first Orion with Lady Chantelle, then Oliver in the rear.

Alex was busy thinking.

She wanted to ask Oliver who the royal family was that had visited Paixor. She needed to know; after all, once she returned to the Summer Castle, there would begin the many royal visitations from the neighboring lands. She wanted to know who she could trust; and if she couldn't know that, it was better to know who she couldn't trust.

But she could not ask without a reason, and she had none that she could give to Oliver that he would accept at the moment. She could not yet tell him who she was; though he was closer to accepting her as a gypsy, he was not there yet.

When they stopped at a stream to let the horses take a drink, and to stand and stretch their own weary muscles, Orion caught her arm and pulled her aside.

"Best let Oliver take the lead. Though he is allowing you to be in front right now, he is not happy about it."

Alex nodded. She had been waiting for Oliver to move in front.

"Alex..."

"I am sorry for this morning. I should not have walked off like that, putting us behind Oliver's schedule."

"We are so far off Oliver's schedule, it hardly matters now."

"It matters quite a bit, actually. I had only a month. We have been gone two weeks now."

"A month?"

Alex nodded. "One month. I must return, or I might lose the throne."

Orion stared, flipping his hands into the air. "And you are just telling me this now?"

She shrugged. "It is my problem, Orion. Not yours."

"We could be far enough away that you cannot return in time."

"We are not so far away, Orion." Alex smirked at him and jabbed him gently on the shoulder. "Not if we travel as the crow flies."

Orion stared at her only a moment before laughing, his shoulders losing their stiffness of only moments before. "I suppose not."

"He is coming around." Alex nodded at Oliver, who stood with the horses. Lady Chantelle could be heard in the nearby bushes, Oliver staring pointedly in the opposite direction.

"Yes." Orion looked at his friend. "I was not sure he would."

"I think I will be able to tell him who I really am before we must return."

"Aye." Orion nodded.

Alex watched Orion, weighing her words. "Will you?"

Orion flinched, looking away at nothing. "Will I what?"

"You know what I am asking."

Orion turned to look at her. "I do not know."

"He may yet come around enough for that."

Orion sighed. "Perhaps. I am beginning to doubt it, though."

Alex bumped him with her shoulder. "Have faith. He has come farther than I thought he would after those first days."

Orion nodded.

Lady Chantelle emerged from the forest, brushing dead leave and twigs from her skirts.

"It is time to be off again."

Orion caught Alex's arm once more, turning her back to him.

Alex smiled. "I already said that I would let Oliver lead now. Should I apologize for overstepping myself?"

"No, that will only make it worse, I think."

Orion did not let go of her arm. "What?"

"Let Lady Chantelle ride your mare."

Alex looked at Orion. "Why? She has been riding her most of the time. She is in skirts and must pull them up to ride safely." Alex snickered. "Aren't you enjoying the view of ankles?"

"What? No!" Orion's cheeks flushed pink. "I just... I am uncomfortable with her riding with me. I would prefer it be you."

"Orion..."

"Please. When the dragon is near, I am warmer. You know this and will understand. She would not."

Alex nodded, swallowing the disappointment that it was not another reason that he wanted her to ride with him instead of Lady Chantelle. "Should I let her know, or will you?"

Orion glanced at the blonde. "Let's just get on my horse and I think she'll figure it out."

"Okay." That was not the best plan, but Alex didn't tell Orion that. If Lady Chantelle thought he was rude, that was all the better.

Once Orion had gained the back of the horse, Alex held out a hand. Orion took it and pulled. The large brown mount didn't flinch when Alex settled behind the saddle.

Lady Chantelle frowned, standing next to the white mare.

Oliver snorted. "I thought Lady Chantelle was riding with you today?"

Taking a breath, Orion stiffened. "Well..."

Snickering, Alex waited for him to offer an explanation. None came. Sniffing hard in his ear, Alex leaned to the side. "Sir Oliver, Lady Chantelle is wearing a dress. It is easier to keep the skirts over her knees if she isn't wedged behind someone else."

Mouth agape, Oliver glanced over the long skirts of Lady Chantelle's dress, then at the horse and saddle. "Oh, well, I guess I can see that. Well, come on." He herded the blonde toward the mare.

"But-" Lady Chantelle stumbled. "I don't think-"

"Look. We can't stay here all day. I want to cover some ground today. Get on the mare and we can get started." Oliver squatted next to the mare, cupping his hands to offer her foot a boost.

Lady Chantelle placed her boot in his palms and grasped the edge of the saddle, glaring at Alex from over her shoulder. She swung one leg over the horse's back, bending forward to inch herself into the seat and tug her skirt evenly behind her so that it didn't bunch. It was not graceful or ladylike, and Alex had to bite her tongue to stop laughing out loud.

"Let's go." Oliver ignored Lady Chantelle's awkward movements, and gained the back of his own horse.

The white mare moved to follow Oliver's mount, though Lady Chantelle wasn't prepared, and fell back in her saddle, only her tight grip on the reins keeping her astride. The jerking caused the mare to flip her head in retaliation and buck.

"Whoa." Orion caught the mare's lead and stopped her instinctive bolt. "Keep control there."

"I'm not the most accomplished at riding this way. I learned on a side saddle." Lady Chantelle stuck her nose in the air and sniffed, hauling her skirts down over her knees. She flapped the reins and the horse started forward again.

"We're wasting time!" Oliver growled from ahead. "Let's go!"

CHAPTER TWENTY-ONE

They traveled in silence most of the morning, Oliver leading, keeping a brisk pace. Lady Chantelle, on the white mare, bounced behind, whimpering at each hard bump in the saddle.

Orion and Alex brought up the rear, riding in comparative comfort, though Alex tried to keep a few inches distance from Orion's back. When she brushed against him, her stomach clenched and it was hard to think of anything but him.

"There's a village up ahead." Oliver stopped, looking back.

Orion increased to a trot to catch up, stopping abreast of him. "We should go in, ask questions. Maybe they've seen this dragon."

"Maybe they haven't." Oliver huffed.

"Who cares?" Lady Chantelle groaned. "I need out of this saddle. And I'm hungry. Not to mention thirsty. Let's see if they have an inn and we can have some tea."

"This isn't a pleasure trip, Lady Chantelle. We're on a mission."

Sighing, the young lady sent Oliver a sharp look. "Fine. Can I at least get a break from the saddle? I'm not sure I'll be able to walk."

Oliver snorted, but urged his horse forward, toward the smattering of stone cottages that heralded the start of the village. The dirt road traveled a straight line between them, and in the distance, the community well sat squat and round in the center on the town square. Chickens scattered at the approaching horses, and a piglet squealed and ran for cover.

Children hovered in open doorways, watching. Women peeked out windows and men lumbered along beside them.

When they reached the well, Alex dropped down to the ground and lowered the bucket, pulling up the water and splashing it into the trough for the horses. While the horses drank, Oliver frowned at the gathering crowd.

Orion smiled and nodded.

Alex shook her head. Oliver was going to scare them off, and they'd never get any answers, let alone lunch or tea.

Lady Chantelle was still on her horse, gripping the reins.

"Orion, Sir Oliver, why don't you help Lady Chantelle down from the mare? I think she could use the assistance." Alex nudged Orion toward the poor girl and approached the nearest villager. "Good day, sir. We are just looking for the chance to rest and water our horses."

"Why are you talking to him?" Oliver rounded on her, tugging his horses reins so that the mount hauled them back so it could drink.

"Because it would be rude not to." Alex turned her back to Oliver, ignoring the young man. Orion could explain.

The villager snorted and sneered at Sir Oliver. "Just rest and water, eh?" The man eyes their bags and horses.

"Yes. And perhaps tea, if you have a place that sells it?" Alex stepped between the man and Lady Chantelle, who was having trouble keeping her knees covered while Orion helped her down. Sir Oliver was ignoring everyone in favor of tending his horse.

"Ye gots the coin to buy?"

"Indeed." Orion answered, grunting as he set Lady Chantelle on the ground. "I have the coin. Enough for a lunch, as well."

"Huh." The villager scratched his chin, his gaze drifting over Sir Oliver. "Where are ye headed?"

"I'm not sure that is any of your business." Sir Oliver turned from his mount.

"Well then, I'm not sure we sell tea."

"Oliver." Lady Chantelle's voice dipped to a whine. "Could you just be pleasant for a moment?"

"I am always pleasant." Oliver glared.

Alex sighed. "Please, sir. We are all tired from our ride and not in the best of temperaments. As Orion said, we have coin to pay."

Orion pulled a sack from his saddle bag and jostled it in his hands. the metallic jingle brought a smile to the villager's face. "Come right this way, then. right this way."

Bowing, the man shuffled off, leading the way to a large, multistory building with a wide chimney. Smoke billowed from the stone tube; someone was keeping a roaring fire stoked in its hearth.

Lady Chantelle groaned, but followed the man, limping and dragging one foot. Sir Oliver walked next to her, matching his gait to hers, hands braced to catch her if necessary.

Alex nodded in the direction of the mismatched pair and winked at Orion. He grinned back at her, shaking his head.

The inn was not crowded, but other travelers sat at long tables, enjoying mugs of mead or ale. Trenchers of roasted meat and boiled potatoes sat before them, daggers leaning against them.

Aromas, enticing to make her stomach grumble, reached Alex's nose. "Perhaps we can get a little more than just tea?" She watched a diner grab up his dagger to spear a whole potato and pop it into his mouth.

Orion looked in the direction of her gaze. "Indeed. I think a full meal is in order. Fresh meat would do much to raise my spirits."

Lady Chantelle sighed. "I should like tea and biscuits and perhaps a bit of cheese."

"Not likely to get such fancy fare here, *my lady*." Oliver snorted and shook his head, glancing around at the other tables. "You'll be lucky just to get the tea."

"I'm sure they have tea." Alex was surprised at the vehemence on her tone. Surely she wasn't feeling sorry for Lady Chantelle. "And I am certain they have something lighter available."

In the end, they ordered a pot of tea, a pitcher of cold mead, a trencher of roasted pork and vegetables and a loaf of fresh bread. Alex and Orion made sandwiches, slamming slabs of the pork between thick slices of the bread, while Oliver ate directly from the trencher. Lady Chantelle sniffed, drank her tea and sampled the vegetables and bread.

The trencher was half empty--though it was mostly vegetables left--when someone approached them.

"Travelers, eh?" The man that towered over them was older, with dark hair and a full beard. His cloak was thick and rich in color, though whether it was red or brown, Alex could not tell in the dim light.

"Aye." Orion swallowed before speaking, wiping the juices from his mouth with a napkin. "We are heading north."

"North?" The man leaned on the edge of the table, eyeing each of them in turn, his hard gaze resting on Lady Chantelle a barest second longer than the others. "What is to the north for you?"

"A dragon." Sir Oliver answered around his tea; though he had refused the meat, he enjoyed the tray of sweets Lady Chantelle had requested to accompany her tea.

"A dragon?" The man sat down, inching his chair closer to Oliver. "What kind of dragon?"

"A fierce dragon. One I have heard has been terrorizing these parts."

At his words, the conversations around him fell away and silence reined.

Alex watched the stranger. Something was not right about him. He held an air of authority, and the innkeeper kept his distance.

"Aye." A man at another table thumped his mead against the wooden surface. "There's been a dragon attacking all along the Bristen highway. Been a right nuisance it has."

The stranger sneered at the man. "Hold your tongue, you drunken fool, if you know what's good for you." Two men that flanked the entrance to the inn shifted, and Alex caught a glimpse of honed metal. They held swords.

She looked back at the stranger. He watched Oliver eat and drink, his gaze straying to Lady Chantelle every so often, his eyes narrowing when he did so. This hand gripped the edge of the table.

Lady Chantelle did not notice the man's looks. Her eyes drifted shut, only to jerk open again. She sipped her tea and took up another biscuit, taking a bite, only to have her eyelids drop to half-mast once more.

Orion sat tense beside Alex, staring at the stranger.

Oliver grunted and looked up from the table at Orion. "What was that for?"

Sighing, Orion looked away to Alex.

Alex shrugged. Oliver was oblivious to the danger the man radiated.

The stranger stroked his beard. "I too, am heading north. Would you care to join my men and me? A large group will be safer I think."

Oliver rested his elbows on the table. "You think there is danger to the north?"

"If that is where your dragon is. Dragons are dangerous, yes?"

Oliver nodded. "There is safety in numbers, I suppose. You are not after this dragon yourself, are you?"

"No, no." The stranger leaned back in his chair. "I own the lands to the north. I am returned home after traveling for business, and would be happy to have a threat to my properties removed."

"How happy?" Oliver swiveled in his seat, bracing his hands on his knees.

Orion feinted another kick beneath the table, but missed making contact.

Alex held her breath. Surely Oliver would not be so naive as to think this man was offering to help them? Her gypsy senses were telling her to run away, long and hard and as fast as she could.

But Oliver did not have those senses, and so he took the man at face value, and sealed an agreement with a handshake. They would travel with his party north, and be paid handsomely when they killed the dragon.

"There be two ye know." An old woman emerged from the kitchens, a wet stained apron wrapped around her brown skirts. "There be a white one, what's always been, and now a green one. Heard the talk, I have."

"There is only one dragon." The Lord asserted, pulling Oliver along to the door. "Settle their bill, Williams."

One of the guards at the door moved toward the innkeeper, hand on the hilt of his sword.

"No charge." The innkeeper squeaked out, his eyes on the sword and not the man's face. he backed away, pushing the old woman back into the other room and following. "No charge at all."

The guard stopped, nodded, and turned to follow his lordship. "Come along." He jerked his head for the remaining three to follow.

Orion stood, eyeing the man.

"Let's not make a scene. We can't protect Lady Chantelle right now." Alex nodded to the girl, who sat upright in her chair sound asleep.

Nodding, Orion tugged the front on his tunic down and circled the table to the sleeping girl, picking her up over his shoulder with a grunt. "She doesn't look it, but she's a lot heavier than you."

Alex raised a brow but said nothing, following them out the door.

The guards brought up the rear, swords now on gleaming display. Outside, Oliver stood with the stranger, laughing and motioning to their horses. They shook hands once again, and Oliver made for their mounts, seeming eager to get started once more.

"I don't like the feeling of this." Orion staggered under the burden of Lady Chantelle's limp form.

"Me either. Maybe we'll have a chance to bolt once we're out on the road." Alex patted down her mare, glancing at where Oliver sat astride his horse, next to the stranger on his.

"Not with Lady Chantelle out cold. We'd never get very far." Orion stood next to his horse, eyeing the saddle and then looking to the limp form over his shoulder. "How do I get her on the horse?"

"Maybe we should wake her up?" Alex lifted strands of long blonde hair, bending to catch sight of the girl's face. Lady Chantelle's eyes were closed, her mouth open and slack. "Or not."

She met Orion's gaze and they shrugged in unison.

"I'll just drape her over the back I guess."

"It won't be comfortable for her." Alex felt honor-bound to point that out, though she moved to the other side of the horse to help arrange the sleeping girl.

Orion snickered. "It won't be comfortable for me. How am I supposed to hold on to her?"

"I suppose we could drape her over your lap."

Orion froze. "No. She's on the back or nowhere."

"Okay." Alex rose on tiptoes to look at him across the back of the horse.

He glared at her. "Haven't you figured out I don't like riding with her?"

Alex frowned. "I thought it was the heat?"

Shaking his head, Orion pushed the sleeping Lady Chantelle closer to the saddle. "Maybe we could strap her on?"

Swallowing hard, Alex made a quick decision, and shook the girl.

Lady Chantelle moaned, and her eyelids fluttered, but she didn't wake up.

"What's the problem?" Oliver looked down from his mount. They hadn't noticed him ride over, so intent on securing Lady Chantelle.

Orion turned to his friend, huffing. "We can't wake her up, and you've been too busy with your new best friend to notice and help."

"What do you mean, you can't wake her?"

In answer, Alex shook her again, and once more, Lady Chantelle's only response was a moan and eye flutter.

"Maybe this lord has a wagon?" Orion aimed the question at Oliver, glaring and gritting his teeth.

"I doubt it. I suspect he's traveling light."

"Could you ask?" Orion pointed.

Oliver followed his finger and spurred his horse toward the man and his soldiers.

"Someone should ride with her." Alex pushed hair back from Lady Chantelle's face. "To answer questions in case she wakes up."

In truth, she wasn't sure how safe the girl would be in a wagon with the soldiers, but she wasn't certain it was a concern that should be voiced aloud with those same soldiers within hearing range.

Orion glanced at Alex after seeing the lord gesture toward a small covered cart filled with sacks. "You have your blade?"

"Always." She stomped her foot on the ground, reminding of where she kept it.

"I'll ride next to the cart, but there is no guarantee that I'll be able to maintain that position. Leading your mare should help."

Alex nodded. "Tell them the horse belongs to Lady Chantelle. That way, me riding won't seem suspicious."

Orion nodded and pulled the girl back onto his shoulder. Striding to the cart, under the watchful eye of his lordship, Alex thought she might be sick. Something was wrong, and everything inside her screamed it, but making Sir Oliver believe it was not possible.

CHAPTER TWENTY-TWO

They rode all day with Lord Salomon's men surrounding them and the wagon. Sir Oliver grinned and joked with them, and they seemed to respond in a similar manner.

But to Alex's eye, there was a difference.

The soldiers laughed too loud and too often. Sir Oliver just wasn't that funny.

Orion sat quiet on his horse, watching, frowning. Alex tried to catch his gaze but could not. He ignored her every attempt.

Frustrated, Alex examined the scenery, and realized they were heading in the direction of the summer castle, which might be an unexpected benefit. Her time was running out if she wanted to keep control of the throne.

Of course, just because they were heading in that general direction, didn't mean that was where they were going. Salomon was not a name Alex remembered; and she had been told the names of all the lords with property holdings near the castle.

The mare pranced beneath her reins. That caught Lord Salomon's attention.

"You seem well-adapted to handling your mistress' animal."

Alex tipped her chin. "Of course. I am tasked with exercising it when she is unable to ride it."

"Indeed. I do not remember her mentioning such a horse when I visited her father." Lord Salomon narrowed his suspicious gaze.

"Perhaps, you should have spoken to my mistress instead of his lordship." Alex's stomach clenched. She just knew the man was going to suss them out.

"I do not remember you, either."

"Most never remember the help."

Alex let out a long breath when the lord motioned his horse into a gallop and sprung to the front of the group.

Orion dropped back. It seems that thought Alex could not catch his attention, Lord Salomon had. "What was that about?"

"I think Lord Salomon suspects something is not right with our group, and is trying to figure out what it is."

Snickering, Orion shook his head. "He will never learn all of our secrets, there are just too many of them."

"Perhaps. But his is suspicious, and I fear that does not bode well for us."

"I fear you are correct."

Orion rode next to her the rest of the ride, though they did not speak. A soldier had also dropped back after a nod from Lord Salomon, and stayed with them until his lordship raised his right hand and hollered "Halt."

As if one, the soldiers all stopped, Sir Oliver a beat behind, Orion another beat, and Alex even slower, almost riding into the back of the horse in front of her.

"We will make camp here." Lord Salomon swept his arm around, indicating the side meadow that stretched to his right. He pointed at the ground beneath him. "My tent, here."

Soldiers scrambled from their mounts, some taking the horses to keep them from wandering while two men erected a makeshift corral from limbs and rocks. Others unpacked the horses and the wagon, first setting the main tent where Lord Salomon still sat on his steed.

Orion dismounted and held Alex's reins while she jumped to the ground. "I will keep our cattle separate from theirs."

"I think that a good idea." Alex scanned the rest of the field. "Not too far away, though."

"Okay." Orion led their horses to a small stand of trees, tying them off loosely before removing the saddles and blankets.

Sir Oliver rode over, frowning, as usual. "Why is Orion putting the horses over there?"

"The mare doesn't like herds."

"Oh." Sir Oliver accepted her answer and rode over to tie his own horse to the trees where Orion was brushing down the two already there.

"That was easy."

"What was easy?" Lady Chantelle was pale but standing on her own feet.

"Convincing Sir Oliver to keep our horses separate." Alex looked the young lady up and down. "You are better?"

The girl shrugged, her golden knots bouncing around her shoulders. "I believe so."

"How was the wagon?"

"Crowded." Lady Chantelle shot a glance in the direction of the scurrying soldiers. "And smelly, like too much sweat and sour wine."

"How are you feeling?"

The lady shrugged and glanced toward Lord Salomon. "I don't want to be here."

"So I gathered." Alex looked toward the pompous lord herself.

The man laughed at something said, throwing his head back and placing his hands on his hips.

"He is, loud, yes?"

Lady Chantelle nodded and stared at Alex. "Do we have to stay?"

Alex glanced toward the horses and Orion, now alone again and staring after his friend, who was striding toward Lord Salomon. "I don't think we have a choice. But, I'll see what I can do."

"Thank you."

A soldier marched toward them, hand on the hilt of his sword. He stopped in front of them, his boots kicking up dust. "Lord Salomon has offered you his smaller tent, m'lady." He bowed to Lady Chantelle.

Lady Chantelle looked over to where Lord Salomon stood talking to Sir Oliver. The smaller tent was set a few yards from his large tent, the soldier's tents and bed rolls arranged in a wide circle around the encampment. "Tell him I am grateful for his generosity."

"Very good." the soldier clicked his heels and spun around to march back to his lordship.

Lady Chantelle did not look happy with the situation.

"Let's make the best of it, eh? At least you'll be inside for the night."

"I'd rather be outside sleeping in a thunderstorm." Lady Chantelle grimaced and walked toward their assigned tent. "Well, let's take a look at what we have."

CHAPTER TWENTY-THREE

"Let's not mention that I'm a prince, okay?" Orion bent down close to whisper in Alex's ear. "Let Lady Chantelle know and I'll try to get the word to Sir Oliver."

"Okay." Alex brushed a stray curl away from her forehead and squinted at Orion. "But why?"

"I don't trust the bloke. For all I know, he might try to get a ransom out of my father for me."

"A ransom?" Alex frowned and glanced to where Sir Oliver was monopolizing the lord. "Wouldn't he need to kidnap you first?"

Orion sighed. "He seems to have made a favorable impression on Sir Oliver. He could just send a messenger to my father, who wouldn't know any better."

"Okay. I'll let Lady Chantelle know."

"Where is she, anyway?"

"Hiding inside the tent Lord Salomon is letting her use." Alex nodded in the direction of the smallish shelter. "She really doesn't want to stay."

Shaking his head, Orion glanced to his friend once more. "I will work on getting Oliver to decide to leave. It won't be easy, though."

"He's rather taken with his new friend." Alex rolled her eyes.

"Be nice, Ally."

"Alex." She hissed the reminder.

Orion winked and strolled in the direction of Sir Oliver.

Alex sniffed and spun around to stalk back toward the tent and Lady Chantelle. "He's such a pain sometimes."

Approaching the tent, Alex was intercepted by one of the soldiers.

"Where do you think you're going?" He withdrew his sword from its scabbard a bit and stared down at her.

Raising a brow, Alex raised her voice enough for the other girl to hear, even inside the tent. "To see if my lady needs anything. I am her servant, remember."

The soldier sneered. "Lord Salomon wants no one disturbing the lady."

"And I am certain my lady would like me to ascertain that she is well and recovered from her earlier faint."

Lady Chantelle emerged from the tent, holding the door flap up and away. Her face was pale, her hair unkempt, like she'd been running her hands through it endlessly. "Alex. Come here, please."

Alex tipped her nose at the soldier and made her way around him, half expecting to feel the cold blade slice through her.

The soldier let her pass, but she felt his stare in her back the whole way. Alex bowed when she reached the tent, just as she would if she really were the lady's servant.

"Please come in. I need you to help me with something." Lady Chantelle ducked back into the tent and Alex followed.

"Orion doesn't want us to mention that he's a prince." Alex kept her voice low so as not to be overheard.

"A good idea. I don't trust Lord Salomon with that information." Lady Chantelle flopped to the pile of rugs the soldiers had placed to cover the dirt inside the tent.

Alex waited for the girl to pat the rugs next to her before settling down beside her. "Would you like me to brush your hair?"

Lady Chantelle pulled on a knot. "It might be a lost cause. I think we'll have to cut some of these out."

Laughing, Alex crawled to her pack, also placed in the tent, and pulled out the brush. The soldiers must have thought it belonged to Lady Chantelle.

"Let's see how bad it is." Settling back on the rugs, Alex started on the very ends of the girl's long hair, carefully pulling at each knot, until the hair was free from tangles. If a soldier had dared to peek in the door, they would have been assured that Alex was indeed, a servant of Lady Chantelle.

"Lord Salomon knows you are not my servant."

"How?" Alex frowned at a particularly tight knot; maybe she would need a pair of shears.

The girl sighed and shrugged, wincing when the movement shifted her tresses and Alex unintentionally tugged on a knot. "Sorry."

"It's okay." Lady Chantelle ignored the pain and twisted to see Alex. "I just know he knows. It's hard to explain."

Alex nodded, still working on the knot. "Your gut is telling you?"

"Yes. I guess you could call it my gut. My mother would have called it my woman's intuition."

"Gwennie called it the second knowing."

"Gwennie?"

"The woman who raised me. She's a gypsy. I've mentioned her before." Alex waited for the snide comment.

"Oh, yes. I remember. Was she nice?"

"She's very nice."

Lady Chantelle nodded and turned back so Alex had full access to her hair again. "I'm glad you were raised by someone nice."

Alex paused in her brushing, smoothing the hair with her hand. "Weren't you?"

"My mother was very nice. And my father. But when she died, my father hired a nurse to care for me, and she was not so nice." Lady Chantelle tipped her head forward. "She kept a switch in her skirts, and would snap it at me any time I did something she deemed unladylike."

"That's horrible." Alex set the brush down and leaned forward to try to catch a glimpse of Chantelle's face. "The only time Gwennie took a switch to me was when she caught me stealing figs."

Lady Chantelle snickered. "Figs?"

"It was on a dare." Alex leaned back. "A boy in the village wanted me to get caught by the tree's owner, but I got caught by Gwennie instead. I think it was even worse. She made me take the figs to him, and he paid me for them, plus he had me pick more for him the next day. Didn't stop her from taking the cane to my butt, but at least I had a little money."

"I have never had any money of my own."

Alex didn't know what to say to that, and a conversation from outside the tent caught both girls' attention.

"The trunk is secure?" It was one of the soldiers, and by the gruffness of his voice, Alex took him to be older.

"Yes." from the exasperate sigh from the second soldier, Alex took him to be younger and used to being constantly rechecked. "It's secure."

"Lord Salomon would be upset if anything happens to that egg."

"I know, I know. He reminds us every morning."

"He won't be now, not with these guests."

The younger solder snickered and snorted. "Guests?"

"That's what he's calling them."

"Yeah, and that's why he's authorized brute force if they try to leave."

"He doesn't care about the men; just the lady. She's the one he doesn't want leaving."

The conversation continues, but fades as the soldiers move away.

The girls sit, Alex tapped her fingers against the brush.

"He has an egg? In a trunk?" Lady Chantelle's whisper reeks of fear and distaste.

"Okay, yeah. Sounds like it." Alex picked up the brush and tries to finish the other girl's hair.

Lady Chantelle pushes the brush away. "We need to find out if it is a dragon's egg. This might be the man that kidnapped me and put me in that tower. I know Lord Salomon visited my father's holding, trying to court me. But others did, too."

"And the egg?"

"He used it to gain control of the dragon. To help bend her will to his." Lady Chantelle twisted around again, even shifting her legs to fully face Alex. "We need to find out."

Nodding, Alex set the brush aside. "Send me on an errand—make it a loud command. So the soldiers aren't too suspicious when I start looking around.

Chantelle pursed her lips. "How about I ask you to find me something? Like an herb to make medicine?"

"I'd be looking for that in the field or the woods, not in the camp."

"Right." Lady Chantelle sighed and closed her eyes, rubbing her fingers into them. "Let me think."

Alex let her think, her own mind running through the possible items she could be looking for.

Lady Chantelle snapped her fingers. "I know. You're looking for something I lost, like a brooch or ring."

Hopping to her knees, Alex grinned. "Yes. Because you would have lost it since you got out of the wagon, or even in the wagon. Is there a trunk in there?"

"There is a lot of things in there. It was too dark to see, but I didn't see it anywhere else."

"Okay." Alex stood and set the brush back in the pack. "I'll start outside the tent and work my way around, waiting for someone to mention the wagon before I ask to check it."

"Why?" Lady Chantelle stood too, and the taller girl had to stoop just a bit under the slanted side.

"It might be too suspicious if I head straight for the wagon. I'll see if someone else mentions it first."

"Right." The blonde tilted her head. "How do you know so much about this? Lying and pretending?"

"I'm a gypsy at heart. It's how I was raised." Alex waggled her brows and made for the door. "Sit tight and wait for me to come back. They won't expect you to look for anything, not when you have a servant to look for you."

"Okay." Chantelle sat back on the rugs, looking rather put out.

Alex sighed. "Of course, if you come out to look, that could keep some of the soldiers busy. And it would seem more important that we find it."

The other girl grinned and jumped back to her feet. "Shall I order you off to look for it then?"

Giggling at Lady Chantelle's enthusiasm, Alex nodded. "That will be fine. Put a good show on, eh?"

Once outside the tent, Lady Chantelle raised her voice and pointed sharply at the ground in the center of the encampment. "Find it now!"

Bowing, stifling the laughter that bubbled up, Alex scurried backward. "Yes, My Lady, yes indeed."

The arrogant command drew the attention of the soldiers, as well as Sir Oliver and Orion, who both came at a run.

"What's wrong? What's lost?" Orion reached them first.

"What has he done now?" Reaching them a heartbeat later, Sir Oliver glared at Alex's bent head.

Lady Chantelle's eyes grew wide.

"We need to find Lady Chantelle's missing ring." Alex tried to elbow Orion, but he was pushed aside by one of the soldiers.

"What's going on?" The soldier stood tall over Alex.

"My Lady has lost a ring and I must find it." Alex strode off to look for the imaginary ring, hoping against hope that Orion followed.

He did.

"What ring?" He hissed in her ear.

"It's a ruse. We overheard something. I'm really looking for a trunk that might hold the dragon's egg."

"Egg?" Orion frowned and looked around at the ground, like he was looking for the errant piece of jewelry.

"The one the Lord was using to keep the dragon in line."

"Ah."

A ruckus near the tent had them look up. Lady Chantelle wagged a finger in Sir Oliver's face while a growing crowd of Lord Salomon's soldiers hovered around them.

"This may be even easier than I thought." The wagon stood abandoned by its guards in favor of what looked to be an entertaining squabble.

"Hurry. I'll keep watch." Orion kept pretending to look for something in the dirt.

Alex jogged to the wagon, looking at the ground as she did just in case a soldier still watched. At the back, she took a last quick glance around, picked up the canvas flap, and jumped in.

The interior of the wagon was dim; the canvas was thick and coated with oil to keep out the rain, and so also did a good job of keeping out the light. There were barrels of what Alex supposed to be mead or wine, sacks of potatoes and apples, and, in the far corner, a locked trunk.

Scrambling on her knees, Alex bent her head to listen, though for what sound she couldn't imagine. Flushing, she lifted her head and tried to lift the cover; the lock held--and there was no key.

But it was a trunk, simple and sturdy, and must contain something of value to be locked as it was.

Alex sighed and moved back to the opening, only to stop when she heard a light thud. She turned back to the trunk and heard the thunk again, and in the dim light, she thought the trunk moved.

Impossible.

She edged back to the trunk, watching and listening. The thunk sounded once more, and, indeed, it jumped.

Alex reared back. Was something alive in there? Was it the dragon's egg, hatching? Or had it already hatched and a helpless baby dragon was stuck inside?

Yelling alerted her that the squabble had escalated.

She moved back to the flap. It was time to leave before the soldiers realized they'd left the wagon unsecured and remedied the situation.

"Hurry up!" The hiss from Orion spurred her on, and she didn't bother checking before lifting the flap and hopping out.

"I think I found it."

"Good. Here." He handed her a slim silver ring. "Give this to Lady Chantelle before Sir Oliver goes ballistic."

"Where did you get this?"

"It is mine, though I no longer wear it as it no longer fits. I keep it in a small inner pocket of my tunic. It is from my mother's family and I am loathe to part with it, but I think I must under the circumstances." Orion led the way back to the mob that was busy picking sides. "Hey!"

The crowd parted before him and Alex followed in his wake, the cool ring held tight in her closed palm.

"My Lady, I found it." Alex bowed deep and held out her hand, opening her fingers to display the treasure.

"Oh! Thank goodness." Lady Chantelle snatched it up before anyone could look too closely and slid it onto her thumb. "My father would have been distraught to learn that I had lost it."

Alex straightened, only to see a red-faced Lady Chantelle spin on her heel and disappear into the tent.

CHAPTER TWENTY-FOUR

Alex couldn't get back into the tent to speak to Lady Chantelle. She was certain the girl was wondering where the ring had come from, and worrying that its owner would want it back--or tell Lord Salomon it didn't belong to her.

Lord Salomon hovered at the tent, calling in to Lady Chantelle to come out and go for a walk.

The girl refused to respond, and Lord Salomon's face grew red and his pacing turning into stomping. Alex expected him to just barge into the tent and drag Lady Chantelle out, but it seemed he had more restraint.

Some of the soldiers watched the tent, too, and would make to approach whenever Lord Salomon stomped away. When they did, Orion would find a reason to walk over and ask a question.

It was reassuring to Alex that Orion was paying attention, but she wasn't sure it was enough. What if he was distracting one soldier when another gained access to the tent?

Lady Chantelle was not safe. Alex's tense gut told her so. She had to warn the girl.

Stiffening her spine, Alex marched to the tent. The soldier on watch blocked her path.

"I must speak to My Lady." Alex made her voice firm, but not too commanding. No sense blowing her cover. Lord Salomon was a baron, and one day would present at her court. She might need for him to not know her when that happened.

"His Lordship has decreed that no one shall speak to the lady unless he allows it." The soldier crossed his arms and stared down at her.

"I am her ladyship's servant. Surely I can speak to my mistress?"

The soldier frowned. "No."

Huffing, Alex glared at the tent. Surely Lady Chantelle could hear the conversation? Would it hurt the girl to get up and come say something?

The flap stirred and a pale-faced Lady Chantelle peered out. "Please let my servant pass. I am in need of him."

"Lord Salomon has given me an order." The soldier sneered and ran a rude gaze over Alex.

"And I am giving my servant an order." Lady Chantelle looked at Alex. "Get in here, now."

Alex understood that it was an act--or that it better be one anyway--and ducked around the soldier and into the tent.

Lady Chantelle dropped the flap and sighed, offering a wan smile in apology.

"Are you okay?" Alex kept to a whisper, darting a glance at the flap and the soldier just on the other side.

"I have the headache." Lady Chantelle rubbed her temples. "I feel like I might vomit."

"Oh." Alex took a small step back. There wasn't much room in the tent.

Lady Chantelle groaned and sat down, closing her eyes and rocking. "It has been a long time since I got one this bad."

"You get them often?" Alex pulled the brush from her bag and knelt behind the young woman. She held it out so Lady Chantelle could see it. "May I?"

"Sure." Lady Chantelle nodded and winced.

Alex stroked the horsehair bristles over the girl's hair, straightening the first layer, before moving it aside to work on the deeper layers. Such tender brushing had always soothed her when Gwennie did it.

Moaning, Lady Chantelle let her head drop back, her eyes drifting shut. "That actually feels good."

Alex continued the sweeping pulls through the long blonde tresses. "Gwennie used to do this for me."

"Gwennie?"

Darn. Could she never remember? "The woman who cared for me as a child."

Lady Chantelle frowned, but didn't open her eyes. "Right, sorry. What about your parents?"

Focusing on the knots at the end of her tresses, Alex licked her lips. "They weren't able to take care of me."

"Why not?"

"They were lost to me."

"Lost?" Lady Chantelle jerked her hair away, taking the brush with it, and turned to stare at Alex. "How were they lost?"

"They just were." Alex swiped the brush and tugged through the knots, harder than she needed to.

"No need to get rough!" Lady Chantelle pouted but stopped asking questions.

But Alex needed to figure out something and soon. They needed protection, and they needed it now.

CHAPTER TWENTY-FIVE

"What are you doing?" Chantelle's soft whisper was barely audible.

Alex sighed. How much to explain? "I'm going to try to visit somewhere in my mind. I might be able to find something to help us."

Lady Chantelle arched one elegant brow. "Somewhere in your mind?"

Chuckling, Alex debated how much to explain. There wasn't much time. "I know it sounds strange, but please trust me?"

Sighing and nodding, Lady Chantelle settled down next to her, arranging her skirts in a perfect circle around her.

Alex sighed. "I wish I could do that. Do you think you could teach me one day?"

Lady Chantelle smiled, her mouth quirked to one side, and nodded once more.

"Thanks." Alex leaned back against the rug that covered the ground inside the tent. "If anything..." she paused "...too strange..." she paused again "...happens, get Orion, okay? Don't try to wake me up yourself." Alex closed her eyes, only to pop them open again and sit up on her elbows. "Oh, and I'll probably get cold and start shivering. You won't need to get Orion for that. But if you start getting cold, get Orion immediately. Or...if...ice forms or something. Okay?"

Lady Chantelle stared at Alex, her mouth slightly open. "Cold? Ice?" She whispered, glancing to the opening and the men outside.

Alex nodded. "Cold. And ice is bad, really bad."

"Okay. I'm ready."

Alex watched her take a deep breath and fold her hands in her lap. Smiling, Alex patted her knee and lay back down, closing her eyes. *Meredith,* she thought, *the meadow in spring...*

Sunlight bathed the meadow in warmth, dust dancing slowly in the still air, the slight buzz of bees in the distance and the staccato chirp of crickets closer.

Taking a deep breath, smelling the fresh newness of the grass, Alex smiled. "I did it!"

"You did what?" Meredith spoke from behind. "Got yourself into another mess?"

Alex turned, not letting Meredith's sour mood ruin her elation. "No. I got here on purpose."

Meredith took in a sharp breath. "You wanted to come here? Do you need help?"

Alex nodded to the first question. "Yes, I wanted to come here." She looked over Meredith's costume. It was a bit more revealing than usual: the tunic she wore was sleeveless, and showed her arms from shoulder to wrist. Colorful markings decorated the skin of her arms, twisting round each other like serpents.

Frowning, Alex leaned forward to see the markings better.

"You have been trying to come here?" Meredith took a step back, pulling a woven shawl around and up over her shoulders, covering the markings.

Alex stared into her face. "Yes." The lie was easy.

Meredith narrowed her gaze, raking it up and down Alex's form.

"For what reason?"

"I need a lesson in protection."

"Protection?"

Alex sighed. "Yes. How can I use magic to keep intruders from entering a place?"

"'tis not an easy thing. It is advanced magic."

Alex shrugged. "I haven't done any easy magic yet. I seem to keep needing the hard stuff."

Meredith considered her, cocking her head to the side, her long gray hair shifting to the side. Alex could see more markings just visible at the side of her neck.

"What are those markings?" Alex nodded toward Meredith's covered arms.

"They are magic--learned magic. You will have them one day."

Alex looked down at her bare arms. She did not want to cover them with markings. "No, I will not. I will be happy with the magic I have been given."

Giving a rueful smile, Meredith shook her head. "One day, you will want more. You will need more; it will become a craving. You will see."

Alex shook her head, turning to look for the camp. Finding it in the distance, she walked toward it, leaving Meredith to follow at her own discretion.

She sat on one of the stools by the hearth. The fire was not lit, the embers gray and powdery. The flap to the tent hung lopsided, and Alex could just see inside to the colorful blankets that lay on the floor and the many containers that hung from its support pole.

Meredith still stood where Alex had left her, watching from a distance.

Alex waited, picking up a stick and pulling it through the ash at the edges of the hearth. She drew figures that she didn't recognize; many-pointed stars and odd-shaped stick-men. She drew lines between them, spirals around them, and letters from an alphabet she didn't recognize.

Alex looked up. Meredith walked towards her now, slowly, keeping the shawl over her arms.

Alex looked back down at what she had drawn, and understanding bloomed inside her. It was not a warm bloom, but a cool one. It came from her magic. Alex leaned over and pulled her fingers through the drawings, smoothing over them with her palm.

She shivered from the cold that trickled over her. She knew how to place a protection on the tent. She hadn't needed Meredith to show her; the meadow had shown her, all by itself.

Alex glanced back up to Meredith. The older woman was quite close now, a strange smile twisting her mouth. The cold inside Alex shuddered, pooling thickly around her lungs.

Meredith sat on the other stool, smoothing her skirts.

Alex wondered if her legs carried the same markings as her arms. Maybe, Meredith's whole body had such markings, leaving only her face and hands bare and brown-skinned.

"Protection?"

"Yes." Alex whispered the word, feeling the cold inside her gather up into a single place inside. It was an intense cold; like a globe of ice resided inside her.

Meredith smiled. "You will need to let me feel your magic, so I can show you how to direct it. Can you do that?" Meredith knotted the shawl at her waist, then extended her hands toward Alex. "Just like I let you feel my magic that time. Remember?"

Alex watched those hands stretch out, the long fingers with their blunt nails. Where her arms extended from beneath the shawl, Alex could see the markings. They seemed to undulate under the sun, getting darker then lighter again.

Swallowing hard to remove a lump of cold in her throat that would not go away, Alex felt the cold of her magic shy back from those hands. She reached her own hands out toward Meredith, trying to pull the magic out, to extend it into her hands, into her fingers so that Meredith could feel her magic.

A mist circled Alex's feet, the damp cold seeping into her clothing to her skin. She shivered, goose bumps erupting over her flesh. She stretched her fingers out again, and the mist crept upward, thickening, growing.

What the-?

"Ignore the mist." Meredith flexed her fingers and stared into Alex's gaze, the witch's irises near black.

The mist swirled tighter, tendrils wrapping like cords around her wrists.

Alex sucked in a breath and jerked her fingers. A voice in the back of her head spoke to her, quietly, a low hum of sound in her brain. *You already know how to place the protections. You don't need to do this.*

Alex pulled her hands back, clasping them in her lap, tightly wrapping her fingers together. The cold inside her relaxed, flowing outward slightly, easing the lump in her throat. She gasped in a breath, shuddering slightly.

Meredith kept her hands outstretched. "Alex?" She whispered the name, sighing at the end.

Breathing hard, each intake of air a gasp, each outtake a rush, Alex rocked on her stool. Tears smarted in her eyes, liquid freeze running down her cheek.

Her magic was trying to warn her.

"I have to leave." Alex stood, backing away from Meredith, knocking over the stool. She stumbled, but righted herself.

Meredith stood, too, her hands still reaching for Alex, her fingers twitching slightly. "Come Alex, let me feel your magic so I can show you how to make the protection."

Shaking her head, her body trembling, Alex backed away. "I can't do this. I can't do this. I need to go back!"

Meredith sighed. "Alex, you can't go back. Not until you learn how to protect whatever it is you want to protect. The meadow will keep you here until you have what you need." She took a step towards her. "Let me help you."

Alex shook her head again. The cold inside was balling up again, tightening into a hard core of ice. The tears on her cheek froze, the air grew cool; Alex shuddered. "I have to go back."

Then, the ice inside melted, running back to the barriers deep inside Alex. Warmth flooded her, and she closed her eyes to the sun.

"Alex!"

Alex opened her eyes to find Orion leaning over her, shaking her, and Lady Chantelle frantically wringing her hands behind him.

"S'okay. I'm okay." Alex struggled to sit up, pushing Orion back, one hand pressing against his chest.

She felt the whoosh of his expelled air against her cheek. It was warm--too warm. His breath on her cheek held the heat of fire.

Looking into his eyes, she saw the dragon-fire burning in their depths. The hand on his chest registered that his body was extra-warm, as well. She remembered the flood of warmth in the meadow.

"What did you do?" Alex whispered the question, hoping that only Orion would hear.

Orion just stared at her, shaking his head, dragging deep breaths into his lungs.

Lady Chantelle answered, kneeling beside them, her hands still tightly clasped, the knuckles were white. "He blew into you."

"He what?" Alex whipped her head toward the girl.

Lady Chantelle frowned. "It is hard to explain. You were so cold. You were shaking and crying and your tears turned to ice. You said if there was ice to get Orion..." Her voice trailed off. One pale hand reached out to push Alex's hair back.

Sweating now, Alex's hair stuck in clumps to her forehead. "Oh." She still didn't understand.

"He said he had to warm you up. I thought he meant put a blanket over you." Lady Chantelle gestured behind her where a pile of blankets lay in an awkward pile. "I made to get blankets but then he knelt beside you and put his mouth over yours and blew into you."

Alex stared at Orion. She understood what he had done. She also understood why he was not speaking anymore; he couldn't. He had pulled the dragon close enough to the surface to generate heat, and then used that heat to warm her.

Staring at him, Alex could see a glimmer on his skin, the faint glisten of scales. The flame burned deep in his eyes, and heat flared off him.

Yes, the dragon was very close. Maybe too close.

Alex licked her lips, finding them dry and hot. She wiped the wet from her face, mixing the tears and sweat. Her eyes stung.

"Thank you." She took Orion's hand and squeezed, trying to tell him that she knew what he had risked. Still holding his hand, Alex turned to Lady Chantelle. "I know how to set the protection on the tent. I need you to get me some cold ashes from the fire."

Lady Chantelle nodded, glancing once at Orion before leaving the tent in a swish of red skirts. The tent flap fell back into place.

Orion let out a shuddery breath, closed his eyes and lowered his head.

Alex moved to her knees, still keeping hold of his hand. Swallowing hard, she reached out a tentative hand to his shoulder.

Orion shuddered, exhaling hard.

Alex rubbed gently on his shoulder. "You need to get out?"

Orion nodded; Alex could see his throat working as he swallowed.

"Okay. Let me check that the way is clear."

Alex tried to stand, using the hand on his shoulder as leverage. Her legs were like rubber, like they might not keep her standing up. Taking a deep breath, she tugged on her hand.

Orion wouldn't let go.

"Orion..."

He looked up at her, the dragon's heat still in his gaze. Alex couldn't move. Orion tugged on her hand, pulling her back down to kneel before him. He kept his eyes on her face.

His other hand moved up to her cheek, stroking it softly with his fingers.

Alex closed her eyes, concentrating on the feel of his fingers on her cheek. That slight touch sent shivers through her.

She felt his breath—hot--*fire*--on her cheek, along her lips, teasing along with his fingers.

She wet her lips, her tongue touching the soft flesh of his mouth. Hot breath filled her.

Then, it was gone.

Alex opened her eyes. Orion was gone, too.

The tent flap waved languidly, though there was no breeze.

Alex sank down to sit on the floor covering, sighing. Grimacing, she wished, silently and alone, that Orion had kissed her before he left.

CHAPTER TWENTY-SIX

Alex stared at the sacks of ashes Lady Chantelle had retrieved from the fire. She knew what to do, but how to do it without being caught? Could she determine a way to hide the protection spell?

Sighing, Alex stood up. Quickly, she worked a tiny hole in the fabric of the bag, enough for the ashes to fall out in a steady stream. Closing the hole with her fingers, she left the tent.

The camp was mostly empty. A few of Lord Salomon's soldiers sat near the fire, talking quietly among themselves, their weapons resting on the ground beside them. They seemed unworried about the possibility of attack, the frenetic rush of activity gone with Lord Salomon and the men he took with him.

Oliver sat on his bedding, cleaning his sword. Slowly, he moved the cloth up and down the blade, twisting it in the last glimmer of light to catch the reflections in it.

Orion's bedding was still piled neatly near Oliver; he had not yet returned.

Alex glanced to the sky, wondering where he was, if he was okay. Had he met up with the dragon they sought? Or perhaps the villagers? Was he in danger?

Pushing the worry away, Alex examined the tent. It was not a large tent, though it was easily large enough for her and

Lady Chantelle to sleep in. Alex knew that she would not sleep inside the tent though, but outside, near the open flap. They could not allow Lord Salomon to guess that she was female. He would have too many questions. His soldiers might have too many ideas.

She just plain did not trust him.

And from the way some of his men watched him, they did not trust him either.

Certain that she was not being observed, Alex began to walk around the tent, carefully letting the stream of ashes fall to the ground just outside it. Circling it completely, she allowed the remaining ashes to fall in a small pile next to the flap then carefully spread it smooth with her fingertips.

Glancing around once more, she began to trace patterns in the ash, closing her eyes, seeing the patterns she had traced in the meadow. Done, she opened her eyes, keeping her finger in the last of the pattern.

Staring down, she blinked once, twirled her finger, and pulled it straight up.

The ash disappeared into the ground, leaving a faint line of white on the grass and dirt. Moving her hand over the line, she felt the cold from her magic and knew it was working--and that it could not be removed by anyone but her.

Smiling, Alex stood up, dusting off her knees with her hands. Lady Chantelle came to the entrance of the tent, a question in her gaze.

"All set. No one can get into the tent save by the flap. And I will sit guard. Orion and Oliver will likely take their own turns during the night."

"Thank you. I don't know why I..." Lady Chantelle didn't finish her sentence. The girl shrugged and twisted her fingers into her skirt.

The shouting of men made Alex glance over her shoulder. She saw Lord Salomon enter the clearing with a few of his men, some type of large animal strung on a pole between two of them. The men were laughing and dancing, jubilant.

"A successful hunt!" Lord Salomon held his hands up then waved a bloody sword toward the beast.

The soldiers around the fire moved, placing more wood on it, moving the stone circle that kept the flames contained outward to make it bigger. Two heavy posts were sunk into the ground, one on either side, and the cleaned beast strung over the fire.

"We will feast on wild boar in the morning!" Lord Salomon seemed to expect some reaction from his men, and received it. The men, once lounging at the fire, had stood upon his return and now roared, arms in the air, fists pumping.

Alex stared a moment, Lady Chantelle standing silently beside her. "I am very grateful for your protections, though. I am not entirely comfortable in the presence of these men."

Turning to look at the young woman, Alex noted the pallor of her skin, the dark circles developing under her eyes. "But you are not uncomfortable with Sir Oliver and Orion?"

Lady Chantelle shook her head. "No." She looked down at her knotting fingers. "I am quite comfortable with them. I do not fear that they will...I don't know...do...something!"

Alex gave Lady Chantelle a small smile. "You feel that you can trust them. That they are honorable."

Lady Chantelle gave Alex a small smile back, and nodded. "Yes. I feel that I can trust them."

"I trust them as well. Even though I do not get along with Sir Oliver, and I know that he does not entirely trust me, I trust him with many things." Alex frowned. "Though not all things."

Lady Chantelle sighed. "I understand that. Though I trust him with my life, I find that I do not trust him with the life of the dragon that guarded me. I do not think he truly understands what I have been trying to explain."

Alex twisted her lips into a wry smile. "He can be hard-headed, that one."

Lady Chantelle laughed, the sound soft enough that it did not travel far. "That, I think, is an understatement."

"Hey!"

Alex and Lady Chantelle both jumped at the unexpected voice.

Sir Oliver raised a brow at their reaction. "Skittish much?"

Lady Chantelle smoothed one pale hand over her still-gnarled hair. "We were not expecting you to be behind us."

"We were discussing Lord Salomon's men, and that Lady Chantelle is not comfortable around them." Alex watched Oliver's face.

Oliver frowned. "Have they said anything to you, done anything..."

"No!" The word was a frantic rush of low sound, a harsh whisper, followed by a bitten lip and a sigh. "It is just a feeling I have. Lord Salomon, I do not like how he watches me..." Lady Chantelle let the words fade.

Oliver nodded. "I have noticed these looks. I wish..." he swallowed hard; Alex could see the sharp bob of his Adam's apple.

Alex raised one brow.

"I wish I had not agreed to ride with them." Oliver glanced over to the men gathered around the boar. "I did not feel as though I had much choice. I was afraid that..."

Oliver's words were cut off by a shout from behind. He twisted around, his arm shooting out to keep Lady Chantelle between him and the tent.

"My Lord! My Lord! We have seen the dragon! We have wounded it! The green one we have seen flying." One of Lord Salomon's men rode hard into the camp, his horse panting and slavering. He brought the steed up short in the center of camp, dust swirling beneath its hooves.

Lord Salomon rushed to greet the man, his hand holding tight to the handle of his sword, now clean and sheathed at his side. The two met in the middle of the camp; Lord Salomon grabbed the reins, stopping the horse, and the man jumped from the saddle, breathing hard.

Alex watched, her stomach churning, her eyes burning. Was the man speaking of Orion? Had they wounded Orion? She found it hard to breathe and reached out to squeeze Lady Chantelle's arm.

"It was flying, my Lord; taking great rings in the air. Avery shot it with an arrow--right where it is soft from lack of scales!"

"Huzzah!" Lord Salomon raised his fists in the air.

His men did the same.

Lady Chantelle gasped.

"Let us ride!" Lord Salomon ran to his horse, throwing blanket and saddle into its back in a frenzy. "I must be the one to kill the beast!"

Alex turned away, bending over, gagging at the bile that rose in her throat.

Oliver turned to Lady Chantelle. "What?" It was a whisper.

"It is him!" Lady Chantelle grasped tight to the back of Oliver's tunic. "He is the man who put me in the tower! I did not recognize him with the beard and without his cape. But I am sure that it is him! He has wounded the dragon."

Alex wretched again.

The men were quiet around the fire that night. They whispered and glanced aside at their leader, Lord Salomon, who was fuming next to his tent. The man paced, hands clenched behind him, muttering all manner of obscenities.

They had been unable to find the dragon.

It seems that a second dragon had arrived, belching flame and scaring off the men. The darker green dragon had flown off to the mountains, followed by the green and gold.

The men thought it might be a breeding pair.

Alex knew they were not, but she worried that Orion still had not returned to camp.

Lord Salomon had not noticed his absence yet, too caught up in his anger at losing the dark green dragon. He had ranted at his men, striking several about their heads.

Most of his men now left him alone, staying instead in small, huddled groups, one always keeping an eye on their master.

Alex sat cross-legged outside Lady Chantelle's tent, watching the large fire, the boar still slowly roasting on the spit, and the lone figure of Lord Salomon. Oliver had gone in search of Orion.

She thought that perhaps he had hoped to find the trail of the dragon himself.

"Still just sitting over here, eh?"

Alex jumped and snorted. "I didn't know you were back."

Oliver squatted next to her, his eyes never leaving the figure of Lord Salomon.

"I only just returned. I couldn't find Orion." Oliver kept his voice low.

Alex sighed.

"What if..." Oliver licked his lips, his teeth worrying them. "What if the dragons got him?" Oliver was pale, his eyes dark with dark circles under them. He did not look at her.

She took a moment before answering. "Orion knows his way around dragons, Oliver. Remember that."

"Domestic dragons. Not wild ones."

Alex watched Oliver's profile; he still wasn't looking at her. "How much do you know about what happened to Orion?"

Oliver finally looked at Alex. "I know that he was kidnapped by a sorcerer and enslaved by a dragon vendor. Is there more than that?"

Sighing again, Alex looked off to the forest. "He was not treated well. And I suspect that domestic dragons that are mistreated may be more dangerous than wild ones. They feel trapped and will stay and fight when a wild one would likely flee."

"Was he injured?"

"Not by a dragon."

Oliver looked to the ground. "Was he beaten?"

Alex thought another moment, deciding what could be said without giving too much away. "When I first saw Orion, he was more than half starved and had fresh welts and scars on his back."

Oliver remained silent. Then he took a breath, words rushing from between his lips. "That would not have been done by a dragon."

"No," Alex agreed, "they were not. They were put there by the dragon vendor." She cleared her throat, and Oliver raised his eyes to her face. "He was not the only one beaten and mistreated. The dragons kept by the vendor were all malnourished and mistreated."

Oliver stared at her a moment.

"Oliver, Orion has an understanding of what evil is, and fighting for survival is not evil. To Orion, that is just nature's way." Alex picked at the fabric of her trousers. "Just as it is sometimes a way of life to trick and steal for food when no one will let you earn it."

Oliver started, his eyes widening in his face. Setting his lips in a tight line, he stood and walked to stand by the men around the fire.

Alex sighed, wondering if she had gone too far. Perhaps, she should have kept to Orion's story, and left her own for later.

It was dark--and Orion had still not returned--when Alex awoke to fighting. Sitting up from where she had slumped over in sleep, she could see to figures outlined by the dying fire. Firelight glistened off Oliver's blond hair. The other, from the arrogant stance, Alex surmised to be Lord Salomon.

His lordship wanted into Lady Chantelle's tent and Oliver wasn't letting him.

Alex stood, pulling slightly at her core of magic, balancing on her toes just in case.

Lord Salomon pushed Oliver out of his way, and two other figures emerged from the shadows, catching him from behind and restraining him.

Alex narrowed her eyes. She pulled her small dagger from her boot, holding it loosely in her hand.

"Out of my way!" Lord Salomon moved toward the tent, his words slurred and his gait wobbly.

Alex could smell alcohol; he was likely drunk. She had confronted drunks before. She bent slightly at the knees, leaning forward.

Lord Salomon stopped in front of her, leering down.

"I said move!"

"No." Though Alex didn't shout, the words carried to the men who held Oliver. Oliver was struggling against them, but both men were bigger than he was. The men pulled harder at Oliver, but were watching Alex.

Lord Salomon pulled his sword, the blade glinting. "You will move!"

The ashes that ringed the tent began to glow. Alex could feel the cold pushing out from them. The symbols she had marked rose up into the air, spiraling and spinning around the tent.

The cold well inside her reacted, too, pulsing and pushing against the mental barrier that kept it in check. She squeezed her dagger tight in her fist, then released it, flipping the blade into her hand, so that she held it in her fingers instead of the hilt, lightly so that she did not cut herself.

Lord Salomon stood before her, swaying, his sword raised, but not quite pointing at her.

"You will not enter this tent." Alex again spoke low.

Lord Salomon watched the spiraling symbols; they would blur in swift movement, then slow to sharp clarity, before spinning off once more.

Alex could hear Lady Chantelle breathing inside the tent; the sound was harsh, like that of a cornered animal preparing to fight. She could picture the blonde, sitting on her palette, listening and afraid.

The cold inside bubbled up, bombarding the barrier. Alex did not want to use her magic unless she had to. It was the same for her dagger. She had it ready, but would rather be able to place it back into the sheath concealed in her boot, unbloodied.

"Do you know who I am?" Lord Salomon sneered.

Alex smirked. "Do you know who I am?" The words were spoken softly, barely a whisper. She let the cold seep into her blood, into her arms and hands and fingers.

Lord Salomon barked in laughter. "You are a gypsy servant. I could cut off your head and no one would care."

"Leave her alone!" Oliver had freed himself from one of the men, who now lay unconscious on the ground, blood trickling from his head to the sand beneath it. The other was working to draw his sword. "Leave them both alone!"

Alex was a bit surprised that Oliver seemed concerned for her as well as Lady Chantelle, but did not have time to dwell on it. Though Oliver had only one of Lord Salomon's men left to contend with, he had no weapon and the man now had his sword pointed at his chest.

"Honorable men protect women; they do not attack them." Oliver shouted, but watched the man with the sword, keeping his distance but unable to come to Alex's aid as it would mean turning his back on the sword.

"But I am not attacking a woman, I am attacking a gypsy boy..." Lord Salomon breathed out harshly. "Ah. You are not a young boy, are you? You are a girl. That is why you are allowed in the lady's tent." Lord Salomon laughed. "'tis an easy solution, then. I will amuse myself with the gypsy girl and leave the lady alone."

Lord Salomon reached out to grab Alex. Oliver shouted "I said to leave her alone!" And turned his back on the man with the sword.

Alex threw the dagger, burying it deep into the shoulder of the man chasing Oliver. The man cried out, dropping his sword, his hand moving to his shoulder.

Lord Salomon pulled on Alex's arm and she fell to her knees, crying out as he twisted her arm. She let loose the cold of her magic and Lord Salomon bellowed in pain. The man reared back, throwing his head aside to scream.

Reaching them, Oliver grabbed Lord Salomon's sword arm and yanked it back—hard enough that his shoulder crunched and popped. Lord Salomon bellowed once again and dropped the sword. But he did not let go of Alex.

Oliver picked up the sword and brandished it at Lord Salomon, but more of his men, awakened by the noise, were coming to his aid, their own swords pulled and ready.

Lord Salomon dragged Alex to him, pulling her back to her feet. She could smell his foul breath tinged with the odor of strong mead. "Come little girl, I am sure you know how to please a man, eh?"

Alex tried to pull her arm away, turning her face away from Lord Salomon's. She could feel his hot breath on her neck and then the touch of his lips and teeth.

She let loose her magic, uncaring of who saw and the damage it might do. But she was afraid, and the magic receded. Locking itself back inside her.

Whimpering, Alex tugged on her arm. Her dagger was gone and Oliver was busy keeping Lord Salomon's men at bay.

"Leave her be!" Lady Chantelle was breathless and struggling to pull Lord Salomon away from Alex. The lady pounded on his back and pulled at his hair.

But Lord Salomon batted her away like a fly and Lady Chantelle landed on her bottom, her skirts tangling in her legs.

"Let her be!"

Lord Salomon laughed again. "Fear not, dear lady, I am sure there is enough of me to go around."

"Not when I am done with you."

Alex gasped at Orion's voice, trying to turn to see him.

Lord Salomon spoke again, and though Alex could not see him, she could hear the sneer in his voice. "With what? You have no weapon."

Orion laughed, the sound lighter than Lord Salomon's. "I have a very big weapon. A weapon sharper than your measly sword--five of them, actually. Five for each hand."

"Orion!" Oliver still struggled against several of Lord Salomon's men. "Help us!"

Alex felt the heat, waves of it washing against her. Lord Salomon released her, shouting out in surprise. Finally free, Alex turned her head to watch Orion finish the change into a dragon; the green and gold scales and the fire burning in the depths of his eyes.

Oliver and Lady Chantelle both gasped; Lord Salomon's men retreated, backing away, their swords raised in front of them.

A flame of fire shot from Orion's mouth, heating the blade in Lord Salomon's hand so that it glowed and he dropped it.

Quickly, Alex scooted away from Lord Salomon, gaining her feet and pulling Lady Chantelle to hers. Keeping back from Lord Salomon, Alex gestured to Oliver.

Oliver came to her, taking Lady Chantelle's arm, holding her upright.

"I'll get the horses ready. I think it is time we left." Alex nudged Lady Chantelle into Oliver's arms.

Oliver nodded, his eyes never leaving Orion. The dragon's head was low, its front claws gouging the ground and smoke wafting from its nostrils.

Alex ran to the horses. Lord Salomon's men ignored her, their attention also captured by the dragon spouting flames.

"Oliver! Chantelle!" Alex forewent all niceties. There was not time. They could be angry at her later for forgetting her manners. "Come on!"

The horses stamped their feet, agitated at the noise and flames. Though they were likely used to the smell of dragon that Orion carried, they were not used to it being so strong.

Oliver dragged Lady Chantelle behind him, heedless of her skirts. Part way to the horses, he simply picked her up and carried her, running as fast as he could. He pushed her up into the saddle of the white mare, and Lady Chantelle hitched up her skirts to her knees, riding astride without complaint, uncaring of who was watching.

Oliver slapped the back end of the horse, "Go!" He grabbed his own reins from Alex and watched as she struggled to gain Orion's stallion. It was taller than her mare by several hands.

Squatting, Oliver grabbed her calf and hoisted her up. Alex flung her leg over and spurred the horse forward, knowing that Oliver would soon follow.

And he did, his own horse thundering behind her.

Orion roared, and Alex glanced back, seeing flames shoot into the sky. She could hear Lord Salomon's men screaming. Biting her lip, she prayed that Orion would not be hurt and turned ahead to watch for Lady Chantelle on the white mare.

CHAPTER TWENTY-SEVEN

They rode hard all night, pushing the horses as fast as they could, stopping only to listen to the quiet, to listen for the sounds that would indicate that Lord Salomon and his men were following them.

But they heard nothing.

Alex listened for the whoosh of wings that would tell her that Orion was flying above, but she never heard that either.

They made camp in the morning, the sun just peeking over the treetops, finding a small copse of trees in a meadow cut by a meandering stream.

All three horses were breathing hard and the white mare was limping, staggering even when they stopped. They animals drank heavy from the stream, then moved to stand in the shade. The mare lay on the ground, rolling to her side.

"Damn." Oliver bent over the horse, examining its leg. "She's in bad shape."

Alex stood behind Oliver and slightly to his left, looking down at the shivering mare.

"I'm not sure that I know what to do for her." Oliver stood, hands on his hips, still looking down.

Lady Chantelle sobbed. She had her hand over her mouth and tears rolling down her cheeks. "I'm so sorry. I'm so sorry."

Oliver pursed his lips. "It's not your fault. We ran all the horses hard getting away from Salomon and his men."

Lady Chantelle continued crying.

Alex looked down at her horse. "What's wrong with the leg?"

Oliver sighed. "She must have stumbled when running. She's got a fracture in the bone, most likely, and if she walks on it, it will likely break through." Oliver sighed again, turning away from the mare. "I don't have a weapon to take care of her."

Alex spun around. "Take care of her? Why would you need a weapon for that?"

Oliver looked at her, his eyes dark and sad. "To put her out of her misery. She's in pain, she can't walk and we can't leave her here. It would be best if we..."

Alex spun back to the horse, kneeling next to her head. "We aren't going to kill her. I can..."

"Hey."

Alex hadn't heard anyone approach and started at the quiet voice. "Orion!" Jumping up from beside the mare, Alex ran to him, into him, wrapping her arms tight around his middle, burying her face in the soft flesh of his neck.

Orion's arms went around her, too, warm and strong and steady.

Sniffing, Alex pulled her face back, hiccoughing and realizing that she was crying. "I was so worried. You didn't come and you didn't come and I didn't know if you were alive or dead and..."

"I'm okay. Shh, Alex, I'm fine. Salomon and his men are running around trying to gather their horses and regroup. I don't think they'll be coming after us anytime soon. I flew in the other direction and then headed south, before turning to follow you. I think they are more likely to take off and follow the dragon than you three."

Orion's arms were rubbing over her back and he was rocking her side to side.

Alex sniffed into his shirt.

He hugged her tight, lifting her slightly off her feet.

She snuggled closer.

Oliver shook his head at the pair. "Orion, we need to do something about the mare."

Alex pushed away from Orion and rounded on Oliver. "You can't kill her. I can heal her."

Oliver frowned. "How can you...?"

Orion tightened his hand on Alex's shoulder. "What is wrong with the mare?"

Alex turned to Orion. "Oliver thinks she stumbled when we were fleeing and she has a fractured leg bone. She can't walk on it and we can't leave her here. He wants to kill her."

She caught the eye roll Oliver directed at her and frowned. "I told you, I can heal her."

Oliver opened his mouth to speak, but Orion held up one hand. "Oliver, do you remember when Alex fell off her horse and cut her head?"

Oliver nodded.

Lady Chantelle looked confused. "This was before you rescued me from the river?"

Oliver nodded again.

"And you say she healed the cut." Oliver's voice was low. "I saw...something like that."

"Yes." Orion looked at the mare, still lying on her side and taking heaving breaths. "And she can heal the mare."

Alex straightened, wiping her sleeve over her eyes and cheeks, and strode back to the mare. Kneeling next to her, she stroked down the mare's neck, crooning softly.

Lady Chantelle watched a moment, before walking over and kneeling beside Alex. "I'll stay here and soothe her while you work on her leg." The offer was made softly.

Offered a small smile and a nod, Alex crawled to the injured leg. "Thanks."

Lady Chantelle began stroking down the mare's neck, taking over the soft crooning sounds.

The leg was swollen and the mare held it stiff and straight. Alex reached out to touch it, and the horse shuddered. Reaching deep inside, Alex pulled the cold up and into her fingers.

She clasped her hand around the leg, feeling the cold seep out of her hand and into the limb. She thought about the bone in the leg, saw it whole and unbroken. She got colder, icier.

The mare shivered and neighed.

Dimly, Alex heard Lady Chantelle crooning, sensed Oliver standing a few feet behind her, and Orion, right there, one hand resting on her shoulder, warm against her, reminding her that the cold was only temporary.

The mare moved, struggled to her feet and walked away. Oliver gasped, Lady Chantelle laughed and Alex shivered, pressing the cold back down, pushing hard to lock it away once more.

It was hard. The cold didn't want to recede. She couldn't move. She felt frozen.

Orion wrapped his arms around her from behind and their warmth felt like fire, hot daggers piercing her skin. The warmth spread, a fire across her skin, in her veins, and finally the shivering stopped, and Alex sagged against Orion, warm but exhausted.

"Is she alright?" Oliver stood closer, Lady Chantelle at his elbow.

Nodding, Orion hugged her closer. "It makes her cold, and she needs to warm up after. This made her especially cold, she was almost frozen. Right now, I think she's just tired. She needs to rest."

Alex let her eyes drift closed, relaxing into Orion. She knew that Orion and Oliver continued to speak to each other, and that Lady Chantelle stayed quiet. She breathed in deep, taking in the warm, comforting scent of Orion, and went to sleep.

CHAPTER TWENTY-EIGHT

Alex stood in the dream meadow. It was summer, the sun beating hard down on the yellow-tinged grass. Sweat trickled down from her temple and across her cheek. She wore a cotton dress, the fabric loose about her legs, fluttering in the hot breeze.

In the distance, she could see the small tent and stools, the cold ashes where the fire would usually be burning, but no Meredith.

Alex turned on the spot, scanning the whole meadow.

Why was she here? There must be something she needed to learn.

Thinking about their circumstances, Alex tried to determine where magic could help them. They were already free of Lord Salomon and his men, so she did not need her magic for that. And she'd already healed the mare.

She walked, just let one foot fall ahead of the other, not knowing where she was going. The meadow would take care of it, take her where she needed to go.

It took her to the new path that cut through the pines, opposite of the path she knew.

Entering the forest, one cautious step at a time, Alex glanced back to the main meadow. Meredith was there now, standing in the center, frowning. Had she seen Alex?

Backtracking to the edge, but not stepping full into the sunlight, Alex watched the older woman. She was not happy; she stomped the ground and paced, short wild steps back and forth. She flailed her arms to the sky, shouting something that Alex could not hear.

Her shawl fell from her shoulders, and Alex could see the twining marks on her skin. They seemed alive, twisting as Meredith writhed. They lifted from her, filling the air around her, spinning into a cocoon of dark air.

Alex took a step back. She didn't want to see any more.

Turning, she continued into the forest, following the winding trail. Though the forest was dark, there was no mist to blur her vision, no raised roots to trip her up. It was silent, not even the rustle of animals in the brush.

A lightening in the air marked the end of the path and the start of another meadow. This meadow was smaller, with a small garden and a stone hut in the center. The garden was well kept, and the stone hut in good repair. It looked like someone should be living there.

The squawk of chickens drew Alex to the rear of the hut. Hens pecked the ground for seeds, a lone rooster strutting with the wire enclosure. A sack of seeds sat lopsided at the back door. Alex grabbed a handful and tossed it into the pen; the chickens rushed the offering, their furious pecking making Alex wonder how long it had been since they were last fed. She gave them more, until the hens were no longer interested in eating.

The cottage was inviting, so she stopped to the door, knocking as she'd been taught. Gwennie had instilled courtesy and politeness in her and discovering she was a princess didn't change anything.

No one answered, but the door creaked open. She pushed it farther in, glancing around the neat room inside. Logs were stacked in the fireplace, unlit but ready. A small table with two squat chairs sat beside it, a rocking chair in the other corner, a red afghan draped over the back.

It was an inviting scene and she stepped inside. Books rested on the shelves of a small cabinet, the spines facing out. Too far away to read the titles, Alex stepper closer, running her fingers down the closest to her.

Her fingers tingled and she stilled the movement. The tingle moved down her arm, into her chest. It was a warm tingle and she was not afraid. Pulling the book out, she opened it, walking to the rocking chair to sit and take a harder look.

The words were hand-scribed on the pages, the scrawl at first long, with sharp edges, but then it changes after about twenty pages, to a shorter, loopier script. Even farther in, the pages bore a rough, print-like writing. It was obvious to Alex, the book had several authors.

She flipped back to the first page and began to read.

It seems, Meredith had told her the truth, she was not the first to visit the dream meadow, and that she was the most recent in a long line to hold the magic within her. And these were their words to those who followed them.

Impatient, Alex skipped to the end of the book, perusing the last pages. What had Meredith written?

Nothing, it seems. The last scribe to put pen to paper was a male ancestor named Saul. She flipped back a few more pages, to the words written by a female in her lineage named Becaena.

No Meredith?

But why not? If Meredith was in the family line, why had she not continued the book?

A sharp wind blew and the door slammed the door into the wall, rattling the books in the cabinet. Alex jumped from the chair, setting the book down behind her. Cautious, she stepped forward, listening.

Another gust of wind hit the cottage, swirling through the windows, whipping the curtains in a fury.

It was time to leave.

The shutters on the window slammed closed, as did the door. the flue on the chimney clanked shut and the interior dimmed.

Outside, a storm slammed the hut, but not a drop of water made it inside. Hail drummed against the roof, but Alex only listened, lighting a lamp to keep reading.

Settling back down in the chair, she rocked in time with the howls, before her head drooped forward and she nodded off.

CHAPTER TWENTY-NINE

Alex awoke to the late afternoon sun slanting into her eyes and moaned, rolling away from the glare, burying her face into her blanket. She was warm; almost too warm--she was beginning to sweat.

Sighing, Alex opened her eyes, squinting at the brightness.

"You're awake."

Alex turned her head, finding Orion sitting next to her. Alex sat up, letting the blanket fall away, and shivered.

"You're cold still?" Orion made to stand, but Alex reached out a hand, stopping him.

"I'm fine. I was just a little too warm under the blankets, and now, the air is making me a bit chilled." Alex pulled a blanket up over her shoulder. She frowned. "Where did the blanket come from?"

Orion laughed. "I'm not sure what happened while I was gone, but Oliver has changed. He rode off, found a small village, and acquired the blankets. Acquired a few other things, too." Orion nodded to his left, and Alex followed with her eyes.

Sitting in a pile near what had been a campfire, was a sack of food, a small pot and the utensils needed for cooking.

Alex moved her gaze back to Orion.

Orion raised one brow. "What exactly happened while I was away?"

Alex thought a moment, not at all sure of Orion's reaction to what she had told Oliver. Of course, Oliver now knew Orion's secret, so it might not be that bad. "I spoke to him about you; a bit about how you had been treated by Jasper. Not that you were a dragon, of course, only that you understood about being mistreated and being hungry and how to handle a dragon. He was worried when it took you so long to get back."

Orion looked at his hands, hanging limply between his knees.

"Then I likened to whole bit to how it is to have to steal one's food because no one would let you earn it."

He raised both brows at that.

"I figured I'd overdone it a bit. He got mad and stalked off to the fire."

Alex sat up fully, letting the blanket fall away again. She was no longer overheated so the cool air no longer made her shiver. She looked around the meadow. "Where is he?"

"He and Lady Chantelle have gone for a walk. Oliver was a bit disturbed, I think." Orion licked his lips.

"How is he taking...well, about you being a dragon?" Alex whispered the question.

"He hasn't mentioned it, though he's been staring at me a lot. He's been rather quiet after returning from his mission for supplies."

"What about Lady Chantelle?"

Orion laughed. "She's been hanging onto Oliver's arm since he got back. I think that might be why they went for a walk."

Alex pushed her hair back behind her ear. "How long have they been gone?"

"Half an hour or so." Orion watched her and Alex found she couldn't meet his gaze. "Are you hungry?"

"Yes." She nodded, still keeping her eyes averted, a blush rising in her cheeks. She thought about how she'd rushed to Orion when he'd arrived, and her tears and anxious chatter.

"Here." Orion offered her a piece of bread and hunk of cheese, and a cup of cool water.

"Thank you." Alex bit into the bread, chewing quickly and swallowing. She then bit into the cheese, still chewing industriously.

"You're welcome." He watched her.

She took a sip of water, put down the cup and finally raised her eyes to his face. Alex blushed all the more. "Why are you staring?"

Orion tilted his head. "Why did you rush at me and cry all over me when I arrived?"

"I was distraught about the horse." Alex looked around. "Where is she?"

Orion nodded to the meadow, and Alex could see all three horses tethered together. "She's all better, though she needs to rest. She was also a bit cold, but she wasn't exhausted like you were and walked it off."

Alex nodded, taking another bite of cheese, though chewing slower now.

"Was it only the mare that you were concerned with? You said you were worried about me."

Alex swallowed. "Yes. I was worried about you." She picked at her bread, crumbling a bit between her fingers. "I was terrified that something horrible had happened to you."

"Why?" Orion stared, intent on her face, the turquoise of his irises brighter than Alex could ever remember seeing them before. "Why were you terrified Ally?"

Alex didn't even care that he called her Ally and not Alex, and she thought, maybe, if Orion wanted her to, she could be Ally--maybe even Alexandrina.

"Hey!" Oliver ran across the meadow, followed by Lady Chantelle, her skirts held up to her knees as she trotted through the grass. "You're awake!"

"Alex! Are you feeling better?" Lady Chantelle, not as fast as Oliver, took longer to reach them.

Alex laughed. "I'm feeling much better!" And happy for the interruption, she thought. Glancing at Orion, though, she could tell that he was not. A frown sank his brows into his eyes, a deep furrow marking his forehead.

"Good to see that you are eating. I did it your way, you know." Alex paused mid-bite, looking cautiously at Orion, who shrugged and stared at the trees. "I bartered a few skills for some of the items we needed, and left some of my coin for others. It is a good thing that I kept my coin purse on me at all times."

"Yes. A very good thing." Alex glanced to Orion. He still stared at the trees.

"I think we should continue on the rest of the day. It is only a little into the afternoon. We do not have to go far or fast, just move." Oliver looked across the meadow. "Though I know that Salomon and his men are not likely to come after us so soon, I think the more distance between us, the better."

"You are correct. I would feel better, as well." Orion stood, dusting himself off.

Alex frowned. "I don't think the mare should be carrying anyone." She stood also, shaking out her blankets and folding them.

"I'll fly." Orion watched Oliver.

Oliver looked uncomfortable for a moment, then nodded. "But keep either very low or very high. We don't want anyone catching sight of you."

"Good idea. One of the horses should be able to carry two of you."

Alex saw Oliver and Chantelle exchange a look, but could not decipher what it meant. Oliver spoke. "I am not sure that is a good idea, Orion."

Orion looked up at Oliver. He had taken one of the blankets and was folding it, but it now hung limp from his hands, one edge pooling on the ground at his feet.

Oliver cleared his throat, and glanced once at Lady Chantelle before speaking. "We rode them pretty hard last night, too. We don't want one of them to turn up lame tonight. Alex shouldn't have to go through the process of healing again so soon."

Alex stopped folding the blanket she was holding, hugging it to her chest.

Oliver went on, shifting lightly from foot to foot. "Perhaps Alex should go with you?"

Orion frowned. "I..."

Lady Chantelle stepped forward, smiling sweetly. Alex wondered what she was up to.

"It would give Oliver and I more time to talk." Lady Chantelle smiled even harder, showing even more teeth. "You know, time to talk...alone."

Oliver started and frowned at her; Orion only frowned.

Alex raised her brows, but Orion seemed to catch on and nodded. "Oh, yes, of course. You two need time to talk. Alex can come with me."

Orion turned and walked toward the horse, handing Alex the blanket as he passed. "I'll fetch the horses for you."

Oliver was staring at Lady Chantelle. "What?"

She elbowed him, keeping the maniacal grin splitting her face.

Staring, Alex wondered at the change in Lady Chantelle. She had no idea what was going on, felt like she had woken up in a world that had been violently shaken and everything was spinning.

She finished packing the blankets, glancing occasionally at Oliver and Lady Chantelle. Oliver was still giving Lady Chantelle strange looks; Lady Chantelle was still smiling broadly and rocking a bit on her feet, humming a little under her breath.

The mare nudged Alex on the shoulder, and Alex turned around, rubbing the mare's nose and cooing at her.

Orion rolled his eyes and Alex stuck her tongue out at him. "You know right well that if your horse had been injured, you'd be fussing all over him now."

"I wouldn't be cooing at him." Orion handed the reins of the other two horses to Oliver. "I'd just make sure his leg was better and let him rest."

Alex snorted. "I just have a better relationship with my horse than you do."

Oliver gaped, the packs in his hands. "It is your horse, isn't it? You didn't steal it like I thought."

She looked to Oliver, still stroking down the mare's neck. "No, I didn't steal her."

Oliver stared at the horse. "You really aren't a peasant, are you?"

Alex shook her head. "No, I am not. Though, I have traveled as a gypsy. Lived with them. Sometimes, I am not sure what I am." She shrugged and nuzzled the horse's neck.

Lady Chantelle sighed. "I think that is something we all do battle with. We are never truly what people think we are."

Oliver was still looking at Alex and the mare. "I'm sorry for how I acted earlier. For what I said. And, well, everything."

Alex nodded. "Apology accepted." She turned back to the horse, stroking down its back.

Orion took a noisy breath, letting it out in a rush. "Yes. Well. We'd best be going or there will be no sense in us leaving at all." He walked away from the horses, giving them space.

He turned back, staring hard at Oliver. "We'll be heading toward that mountain." Orion pointed at a nearby peak. "The other dragon is there, hiding. I told her we would bring someone who could heal her."

Oliver nodded. "I'm not going to harm it. Not now. I...I think I understand now."

Orion grinned at Oliver, and slowly, Oliver grinned back.

"Change in quest?"

"Yes. I think that would be appropriate. I think my new quest is to stop Lord Salomon, who thinks to control dragons and force innocent maids into marrying them. To seek freedom for this dragon he has enslaved."

"I think I like this quest much better." Lady Chantelle batted her eyelashes at Oliver and held out her hand, palm up, to return the ring to Orion. "And this I should return to you. Thank you for letting me borrow it for our ruse."

CHAPTER THIRTY

The meadow was warm, though a cool breeze stirred the curls at Alex's temples. She was wearing a formal dress, which she found odd. She was usually in pants and tunic when she visited the meadow, or the peasant's dress of last time; a cloak and boots if the weather required them.

"Hello?" She called out. She could not see Meredith, and the little camp with the tent looked abandoned.

"Hello."

Meredith lurked behind her. The woman smiled and her hair was unbound from the usual thick braid. She, too, was wearing a formal dress.

"Why are we dressed thus?"

"We must be celebrating."

"Celebrating?" Alex could think of nothing to celebrate, other than that Sir Oliver seemed to value her as something other than a nuisance.

"There must be something. The meadow responds to you." Meredith swept past and walked toward the camp. The trunk was locked and the tent flap closed. The ashes in the fire were gray and cold.

"How long have you been here?" Alex followed Meredith to the camp, picking up her skirt to keep the hem out of the grass. She was wearing dancing slippers.

The older woman shrugged. "I am here now."

"Where were you before? I came once and you were not here."

Meredith stopped next to a stool and spun around. "You came when I was gone?"

"Yes. This is the first that I have been back." She didn't mention watching her in the meadow.

Meredith looked off toward the woods, her eyes narrowed and her lips pursed tight together.

"I did not know how to let you know I was here."

"What did you discover all alone?"

Alex shrugged. "Nothing. I was stuck here with no one to show me anything. I wandered around a bit before someone woke me up."

"You are always asleep when you come?" Meredith sat on the stool, fussing with her skirts.

Alex was happy to see that her skirts did not sweep gracefully to the ground, but bunched up the way Alex's always did.

"Not always before I come, but I wake up when I leave." Alex did not sit, but stood, frowning. "Or waking up makes me leave."

"How interesting." Meredith leaned forward and patted the other stool. "Have a seat. We can chat for a bit."

Taking a seat, she adjusted her skirts, noting how much smoother her own skirts fanned out since watching how Lady Chantelle did it. "What do you want to talk about?"

"How about your plans for the future?" The older woman clasped her hands in her lap, sitting prim on the stool, like they were preparing to share tea.

"The future?" Alex hadn't thought about her future much, so engrossed in the present and what was happening now. "I haven't been thinking about the future."

Meredith's lips pressed together for the barest second, before she smiled and nodded. "Quite understandable. We often don't think about the future until it's too late."

"Too late?"

Nodding, Meredith shifted her skirts, smoothing them. "It is too late when we are old and the future has become our past."

Alex cocked her head, trying to figure out where the conversation was headed. She was not so naïve to think that this was an innocent chat; Meredith had an agenda. "How can the future become our past? What lies ahead is always the future."

Her chest rising with a deep breath, Meredith continued to smile and run her hands over her lap. "I meant, when we are too old to choose the path we want."

Choosing a path. Her words made Alex compare the twisting, foggy trail through the forest that led her to Orion the first time, with the path in the opposite direction that took her to the sunny little hut with the chickens. Though the way had been frightful, Orion waiting on the other end had been worth the trouble.

"Did you choose the path you wanted?"

Meredith grinned and nodded. "Indeed. I made the choice when I was young – like you – and followed that path through to the end."

"The end?" Alex wasn't sure she wanted to continue the conversation.

"The end." The older woman leaned forward, whispering. "To here. Where I am free to use my magic all I want."

Alex looked around. This was the end?

When Meredith placed a warm hand on her arm, Alex turned back. "You are happy here?"

"Oh, yes. I have nothing to fear here."

"But you are alone." Alex thought of leaving behind Orion, and Oliver and Chantelle, her parents and Gwennie. "I couldn't be happy alone."

"I am not alone, you are here." The grasp on her arm tightened, and a stabbing pain shot into Alex, making her gasp and grab her chest with her free hand.

"I don't want to be here." Alex forced the words out; the pain made it difficult to concentrate. It spread through her, tripping along her veins. The cold inside welled up, pushed against the stabbing intruder.

Meredith shuddered and tightened her grip. "You will stay here, Alex."

"No!" Alex wrenched her arm away and stumbled back, picking up her skirts to run. She didn't look back, making her way to the eerie path that had once taken her to Orion.

CHAPTER THIRTY-ONE

A sudden rigidity in Orion alerted Alex that something was wrong. She opened her eyes; he dove down.

Glancing below, Sir Oliver and Lady Chantelle were surrounded by Baron Salomon and his men.

Oliver was off his horse, using it as a shield between him and some of the soldiers. His other hand held the lead for the white mare.

Lady Chantelle was still astride, but was having trouble difficulty controlling Orion's horse. It was shying back and kicking outward at the men.

Baron Salomon had his sword drawn and was speaking to Sir Oliver, who kept shaking his head and backing away, trying to keep the large horse between them.

A shout from one of the soldiers made the baron look upward and Alex knew it meant that she and Orion had been spotted.

In a moment, a slew of arrows shot skyward. Orion banked sharply and they chinked against the hard armor of his underbelly scales. Alex gripped with her knees and hands, molding her body as best she could to Orion's back.

Orion banked again, in the opposite direction, and Alex could see Sir Oliver and Lady Chantelle trying to use the diversion to escape, but Sir Oliver wasn't letting go of the white mare, and the white mare wouldn't run.

The delay gave some of the baron's men time to realize what was happening and they drew their swords, easily trapping Lady Chantelle within a circle of pointed swords.

Sir Oliver raised his hands in surrender and forced to his knees on the ground. Lady Chantelle stumbled from the back of Orion's horse and tried to run to him, but was held back by a soldier who grabbed her from behind, picking her up so that her legs kicked at the air.

Alex tried to pull the cold up from inside her, to tap into the magic core, and *do* something, but couldn't. Her magic was not responding, but stayed a cool blob of energy inside her.

Tears formed in her eyes, as much from frustration as from the whipping wind. Orion twisted in the air, avoiding another rain of arrows.

Another batch flew above them.

They were trying to force him down. Alex tried to tell Orion, but the wind took her voice. The dragon twisted once more, and Alex felt herself slide along his back. She gripped all the harder, digging her fingers hard into the flesh at the base of his wings.

But her right arm hurt. Blood welled from four lines of welts across her forearm; Meredith's nails had left a mark.

Alex knew what it was like to fall off Orion's back; she did not want a repeat performance now.

Orion corrected and Alex rebalanced herself, using her left hand as an anchor.

But they were going to have to land, and with the arrows Baron Salomon's men were shooting at them, it would have to be right in the midst of the soldiers.

Orion banked again, a wide sweeping turn, but a volley of arrows made him sharpen it, and he brushed the treetops, sending branches flying through the air.

Alex slid sideways again.

"We'll have to land, Orion. If we don't, they might hurt Oliver or Chantelle."

Orion flapped his wings hard, pushing them higher, while dipping his tail and stretching out his legs.

He was preparing to land.

The men on the ground seemed to know what he was doing and backed away, creating a circle in the middle of the clearing. Some drew their swords, while others kept their arrows notched and ready.

Baron Salomon watched from the sidelines, his own sword ready, Sir Oliver kneeling beside him, a soldier's sword at his throat.

"Do not bother becoming human." The baron spoke loudly, though he didn't shout. The amulet around his neck glowed red, and Orion shook his head, whimpering. Alex stroked his neck.

"What are you doing?" Alex narrowed her eyes, trying to make out the form of the glowing necklace.

Baron Salomon smiled, but it was not a pleasant twist to his lips. "Demonstrating my power. Your friend will not be able to become human and hide his monstrous form." He waved his arm, and soldiers pulled large chains from a wagon, throwing them over and around Orion, locking the chains together to bind him.

"Get down."

Alex considered resisting, but the men with the arrows moved forward. She slid carefully down Orion's side, avoiding the chains, using her left hand more than her right.

Orion writhed within the chains; the amulet glowed even redder.

"You are hurting him." Alex confronted the baron. She searched again for the cold core of magic and found nothing. She was helpless.

"He is resisting my control. If he would only give in, there would be no pain."

Alex knew better than to think that Orion would give in to having anyone else control him.

Two soldiers grabbed her arms and dragged her forward, forcing her to kneel next to Sir Oliver. The young man's own arms were tied behind his back, his sword taken. They roughly tied her hands behind her, tight enough that the rope drew fresh blood when it pulled along her skin.

Only a day's ride from the Summer Castle, and they were caught.

CHAPTER THIRTY-TWO

Orion bellowed and sent a burst of flame from his mouth, singing one of the soldiers at the chains.

"None of that!" Baron Salomon grabbed Lady Chantelle and held his short sword to her side. "You don't want your friends getting hurt, do you?"

Grunting, Oliver struggled against his own bindings. The guard next to him kicked him and he stopped.

Alex thought she might throw up.

"Change of plan, men." Baron Salomon gestured widely to his soldiers. "It seems the new princess wants a dragon. I think we will see what reward we might get from her for this one." He pointed to Orion.

He fisted Sir Oliver's writ of passage in his hand, shaking it before his face. "What was she offering you for a dragon, boy?" He leaned over Sir Oliver, the amulet's red glow pinking the pair's faces.

"Nothing."

"Do not lie to me, boy." The baron waved the papers over his head. "One does not simply ask for and be given such a writ of passage from the crown on a whim. Why were you looking for a dragon? Why does the princess want one?"

Sir Oliver sneered up at the baron. "I was sent on a quest for information. To determine if the stories about the dragon attacks were true."

"Information, eh?" Baron Salomon lowered the papers and tapped them against his other hand.

"She would not give me permission for my quest unless I agreed to determine the validity of the stories first."

"And if these stories were true?"

"Then I had permission to destroy the beast."

"I see." Baron Salomon thrust Lady Chantelle toward one of his soldiers. The soldier grinned at her, revealing gapped, yellow teeth.

Lady Chantelle shuddered and tried to pull away, but the soldier kept tight hold of her arms.

"Leave her alone!" Oliver struggled in his ropes again.

"Do not worry about the Lady, boy. I will be taking very good care of her." Baron Salomon moved to stand before Alex. "This is the one you need to worry about." He roughly nudged Alex's leg with one booted foot.

"Leave her alone, too!" Oliver pulled at the ropes binding his hands. "She is on this quest at the behest of Baron Castellan."

"Indeed.?" The baron nodded to one of his men and the soldier pulled Oliver's ropes even tighter. "So, Baron Rothschilde is placing spies of his own now? Will wonders never cease." Baron Salomon leaned over Alex. "What is his plan, little girl?"

Though Alex could no longer see Orion--she could see nothing beyond Baron Salomon's face where it loomed over her--she could hear him--the chink of metal and the grunt when the chains pulled tight. Soldiers shouted behind Baron Salomon and Alex could hear the dull thud of weapon against scale.

"Leave the dragon alone and don't hurt us--and I will tell you everything." Alex spoke quietly, staring up at the baron, keeping constant contact with his stare. She took a deep breath; she did not dare give away her bluff.

"Indeed." The baron straightened and waved at his men. "Hold off."

The noise stopped and Alex could hear the ragged breath of the dragon.

Alex glanced at the amulet; it was still glowing faintly. "I would ask for your word, but I doubt it would mean much."

The baron snorted. "I need not give my word to the likes of you, peasant!"

Spittle caught Alex on the cheek, but with her hands bound she could not wipe it away. A soldier laughed. Alex did not move.

"Well?"

Alex moved her cheek forward. "A cloth."

The baron laughed along with his soldiers. "You should be used to such by now, girl. Tell me what you know."

Alex took a deep breath. "The princess is looking for a cohort--one who would become king if he pleases her. I am sure you have heard that Baron Humphrey is hoping to gain that position?"

Baron Salomon smiled and nodded. "Many have been vying for that position. I have heard that since he is one of her advisors that he is near certain to attain what he wants. Many of the barons are wary of him gaining that much power."

"I am sure. Even Baron Rothschilde is concerned. As an advisor to the princess, he holds much power himself; power and influence he does not want to lose."

"Go on." Baron Salomon began to pace.

Alex took another breath. "The princess is, shall we say, enamored with dragons?"

The baron shrugged. "She is young and likely fanciful."

Alex licked her lips. "Baron Rothschilde hopes to impress the princess with a dragon, in the hopes of maintaining his advisor status even after there is a chosen cohort."

"Shut up! Shut up!" Sir Oliver used his entire body to jostle Alex. "Do not tell him anything more."

Alex ignored Sir Oliver and continued to stare at Baron Salomon. "I am sure, if you brought her a dragon, and even showed her how to control it, that she would certainly reward you with what you seek."

Baron Salomon stopped pacing and grinned. "Yes. Yes, indeed. In fact, I am sure that such an impressionable and fanciful young lady would reward me very highly, *very* highly indeed. Perhaps even higher than I had imagined."

Alex stared at the baron, her stomach clenching.

Baron Salomon looked around at his men, sweeping his arms out and up and giving a mock bow. "I do believe that you are looking at the man who will be King of Vreden."

CHAPTER THIRTY-THREE

Sir Oliver glared at Alex from his place in the front corner of the wagon. Lady Chantelle, a slight bruise forming on her cheek, sat next to him, leaning against his shoulder. They were both tied up, hands secure behind their backs.

Alex was in much the same state, only she was sitting as far from Sir Oliver as her bound body allowed.

Their horses walked behind the wagon, tethered by long ropes and flanked by soldiers with swords drawn.

Behind the horses, and flanked by the rest of Baron Salomon's men, was Orion, still in dragon form, still covered in chains.

Baron Salomon and a few of his men rode in the front, leading the way to the Summer Castle.

"You should have kept your mouth shut."

"You will have to trust me, Sir Oliver. Everything will be fine once we reach the Summer Castle."

"Fine? How will it be fine? Baron Salomon will hand over the amulet to the princess and we will likely be thrown in prison."

"We will not be put in prison."

"You think Baron Rothschilde will appreciate all that you told Baron Salomon?"

"I think he will have a good laugh in the end, yes."

"A laugh?" Sir Oliver sounded like his words were strangling him.

"Please..." Lady Chantelle lifted her head. "Can we just stop fighting? There is nothing to be done now. Perhaps my father will be at the Summer Castle and can tell my story. Surely the princess will not trust the baron once she knows what he has done?"

"She will not–"

Sir Oliver laughed. "The princess is a foolish girl playing at being a ruler."

Alex sat up straight. "What do you mean?"

"She has her advisor's making all of the decisions and running the kingdom. She is too busy playing at her fancy dress to bother with her people."

"What do you know of anything? You were in Paixor."

"Please..." Lady Chantelle tried to interject.

"I know enough. Where had she been all these years while her uncle ruled--or rather didn't rule and let everything fall to ruin? She was hiding. She is a coward."

"The princess is not a coward! You know nothing! She did not even know who she was!"

"Oy! Be quiet in there! Or I'll come in and make you be quiet." The soldier waved with sword at them in warning.

Alex sat back against the side of the wagon. Surely no one else thought that about her, did they? Did they all think she was a coward who had been hiding away? Did they all think that she was playing at wearing the crown?

But aren't you?

She ignored that inner voice. But she could not deny that she was off on an adventure instead of seeing to the business of ruling her kingdom. She *had* left her advisors in charge.

Leaning her head back, she hit it against the wood. Tears started in her eyes and she closed them, listening to the faint clink of the chains behind them.

I need to go to the meadow.

And she was there.

It was beautiful, the snow falling gently and just starting to cover the ground, bits of green grass still peeking up through the gathering layer of white.

The tent and the fire were close this time. Alex had appeared almost on top of them. She turned, looking for Meredith, but the older woman was nowhere to be seen.

Sighing, she sat on a stool, picking up a stick to drag through the cooling embers at the edge of the hearth. There was only one stool this time, sitting next to the gray cold ashes from the fire. The pot was suspended over the half-burned wood, nothing inside.

And there was no trunk; just the tent and the stool and the ashes with the empty pot.

A bird trilled overhead, weaving through the falling flakes. It was a red bird, a bright shot of color against the gray and white of the clouds and sky. The bird circled, trilling a disjointed tune.

Alex listened, trying to make out the notes and the type of bird, but she did not recognize it. She had never before seen a bird of such bright color.

The snow fell harder and a colder wind blew through the meadow, stirring the flakes on the ground into little drifts.

The bird kept circling, its tune getting louder and more disjointed. It no longer seemed to be singing.

Alex frowned and shivered. A fire lit in the ashes, its golden flames licking upward to the empty pot. Warmth spread out from the flames, and she leaned closer.

The bird still circled but it was no longer singing. Fat flakes of snow settled on its plumage, dulling its brilliance. It seemed to be struggling to fly, its circles getting smaller and closer to the ground.

Alex stood up and watched the bird get closer and closer, circling ever nearer, until it landed next to the fire.

It looked at her, cocking its head beneath its covering of snow.

"You're trying to teach me something aren't you?"

The bird cocked its head in the other direction.

"What is it?"

The bird opened its beak and let out a raucous chorus that hurt Alex's ears. She had to place her hands over them to block out the sounds.

The bird closed its beak and sat, the snow almost completely covering it now.

Alex dropped her hands.

The birds let loose the horrible sounds once more.

"Stop it!" Alex didn't bother trying to cover her ears.

The bird stopped. It sat, unmoving beneath a pile of snow.

Alex moved forward, the snow heavy at her own feet now, and made to brush the snow away from the bird, but now it was nothing but an empty pile of snow. She threw the snow away, but still there was nothing there.

She turned back to her stool. It too held a small pile of snow, and she brushed it away, relieved that her stool did not vanish as well.

The fire crackled and spit when the snow fell into it, but it did not go out. Steam rose from the empty pot, and Alex cautiously craned her head to look inside. Something was bubbling in the pot now, globes of air bursting at the surface.

"Now what?" Alex wished Meredith were here, that the older woman could help her figure out what she was supposed to do. The meadow didn't seem to be telling her anything about her magic. Not this time.

But it had to be. Meredith had said the meadow responded to her. So, what was it trying to tell her?

Alex fell off the stool and when she opened her eyes she was back on the wagon with Sir Oliver and Lady Chantelle. They were on rough ground and the entire wagon was bouncing. Sir Oliver was still scowling at her.

"Sir Oliver, I am sure that Alex was only doing what she thought was best at the time."

Sir Oliver sat mute, lips pursed, his brows compressed to a single line across his forehead.

Lady Chantelle sighed. She patted the skirts of her red velvet dress; it was awkward, her hands veed where her wrists were bound, and the movement did little to fix the material.

Alex stared at the red skirts and thought how the color of the dress nearly matched that of the bird in the meadow.

We aren't listening to her.

Alex smiled at Lady Chantelle. "Thank you."

Lady Chantelle looked up from her skirts, her hands stilling on the rumpled fabric. "For what?"

"Believing in me. Defending me."

Sir Oliver snorted and shook his head.

Alex shuffled closer, the ropes making her slow and ungainly. She sighed and stopped only half-way across the floor of the wagon.

"Sir Oliver," she kept her voice low, "I lied to Baron Salomon."

Sir Oliver turned to stare at her.

"I told him nothing that would help him, only what I thought would get him to take us to the Summer Castle."

"Why to the Summer Castle? The soldiers there are just as likely to just kill Orion as these ones."

"They will not. Trust me on this. As long as they see me, they will take no action whatsoever against Orion."

"Why not?"

Alex licked her lips and closed her eyes. Would Oliver believe her?

"Huzzah! We are here!" The shout of the lookout soldier spread to the rest of the baron's men, and soon they were all shouting.

"Just trust me on this, please?" Alex didn't bother whispering; no one outside would hear her words over their jubilant noise.

Sir Oliver nodded and leaned back against the side of the wagon. Lady Chantelle nodded, as well, and settled back against his shoulder.

Alex looked out the back of the wagon at Orion, meeting his turquoise gaze. She hoped he understood what she was doing. She'd hate for him to have his own plan germinating, and the two strategies be at odds with each other.

CHAPTER THIRTY-FOUR

Baron Salomon, the wagon and the dragon, along with a handful of his men, were ushered into the castle's courtyard by a contingent of royal soldiers in their formal red and black uniforms. The royal soldiers had their swords drawn and watched the dragon carefully.

The baron laughed. "Do not worry about the dragon, he is well under control. He is a gift for Princess Alexandrina."

"I see."

Alex smiled at the deep voice. She recognized the captain of the royal guard. She winked at Sir Oliver.

Sir Oliver snorted and shook his head. He mouthed his reply. "We are doomed."

"We are not; wait and see."

"Let the barons know there is a visitor to the castle, with a gift for her highness, the Princess Alexandrina." Lord Salomon boomed his announcement.

Alex thought the barons had probably heard him and didn't need to be told.

"Aye, sir." Alex heard the scramble of boots on flagstone and grinned. There was additional movement outside the wagon, and Alex heard Orion shifting beneath the chains and Baron Salomon's soldiers shouting at him to stay still.

"What is going on here?" It was Baron Humphrey.

"Good day, Baron Humphrey. I am Baron Salomon. I bear a gift for the princess."

"You brought her a dragon? Are you trying to assassinate her? Guards!"

"Of course not! This dragon can be controlled." There was a shuffle of boots outside and the clip of hooves on stone. "Is Baron Castellan here?"

"I am Baron Castellan." The Baron approached, eyeing the dragon and keeping his distance.

"My lord, I have brought a dragon for the princess."

"So I see. Why?"

"A peasant spy of yours informed me of the princess's delight in all things dragon and I thought to offer my apologies for not attending her summons by presenting her with a gift."

Alex could see the tightening of Sir Oliver's mouth. She grinned at him, trying to ease his tension. Reaching out one leg, she nudged him with a toe.

It only made his mouth tighten more.

"A peasant spy?" Baron Castellan's voice drew closer.

"A young gypsy girl who dresses as a boy. I believe you sent her on a mission with a dragon slayer?"

"Ah, yes. *That* spy. Where is she now? And those she traveled with?"

Men approached on the flagstone of the courtyard, their footsteps heavy on the stone cobbles. The end of the wagon dipped down and two of Lord Salomon's soldiers came into view. They sneered and roughly pulled her out of the wagon, then grabbed Sir Oliver and Lady Chantelle in turn.

The soldiers pushed her forward, and Alex stumbled, almost falling to the ground but the soldier grabbed her by the arm.

"You may want to consider being a bit more gentle." Alex didn't bother keeping her voice low.

"Why would I do that?" The soldier was still sneering.

Alex said nothing, but turned her gaze toward Baron Castellan and Baron Rothschilde, who had been silent so far. The barons stood on the steps to the great hall, Baron Humphrey two steps down, and all were not looking happy.

A gasp from behind made Alex look back; Lady Chantelle was roughly shoved forward and Sir Oliver was trying his best to help, but could do nothing with his hands still tied.

Movement from the Royal Guard caught Alex's attention then. Those soldiers, dressed in deep red uniforms, were pulling their swords and moving towards the soldier holding her.

She shook her head and they stopped.

"Your spy, Baron." Baron Salomon bowed deeply, the glowing amulet swinging on his neck.

"I see." Baron Castellan's voice was low.

"And, I have this for Her Majesty, as well." Baron Salomon held out the amulet, but did not remove it from his neck.

Baron Castellan moved forward. "I will take that."

Baron Salomon frowned and stepped back, clasping the amulet to his chest.

"It will not go to the princess unless I am allowed to examine it." Baron Castellan held out his hand.

Baron Salomon did not hand it over. "This is a special amulet. It is used to control the dragon. If I give it up to you, the dragon will be uncontrollable."

Baron Castellan glanced at Orion.

Alex knew he did not realize that it was anything but a regular dragon, and tried to catch his eye. She nodded once toward the amulet.

Baron Castellan looked back to Baron Salomon. "It is chained. I am sure it will be fine while I examine the amulet. It should not take long; I must make sure it will not harm the princess. I am sure you understand."

Baron Salomon looked to the dragon, then to his soldiers. "Keep your weapons on them." He turned back to Baron Castellan and removed the amulet from around his neck, holding it out.

Baron Castellan took the amulet.

Alex sighed and smiled. "Baron Castellan, break it."

Baron Castellan looked at her, his eyes wide. "Break it?"

"Yes, break it. Smash it on the stones. Now!" She made the last word a command.

Baron Castellan obeyed, raising the amulet above his head and throwing it to the ground. The jewels were set free from the setting and bounced away, the chain laying bereft at the baron's feet.

The guard holding Alex pulled her back roughly and raised his sword, but two of the Royal Guard pulled their own swords and had them at his throat before Alex could catch a breath.

"Free Sir Oliver and Lady Chantelle." Alex nodded toward her friends, her voice ringing sure and strong in the courtyard. "And get those chains off the dragon--immediately."

The Royal Guard jumped at her words, and Sir Oliver and Lady Chantelle found their bindings cut and Baron Salomon's soldiers unarmed.

"Who do you think you are?" Baron Salomon made to raise his own sword, but was stopped by Baron Castellan's soldiers.

Her own ropes severed, Alex straightened and pushed out her chin, never more proud to speak her entire given name. "I am the Princess Alexandrina Constancia Eliza."

The baron dropped his sword and swore.

"And you, sir, are no longer a baron. Not in my kingdom." Alex relished the sharpness of her words, feeling no guilt whatsoever. It was exhilarating giving commands--and having them obeyed.

Baron Castellan's soldiers grabbed him by the arms and held him.

Alex turned to Sir Oliver, grinning. "Didn't I tell you all would be well, Sir Oliver?"

"Well...I...yes...but..." Sir Oliver was pale and looked like he was going to be ill. Lady Chantelle stood beside him, her mouth a small, perfectly formed "o".

Alex turned back to her advisors. Baron Castellan held the amulet's chain in one hand, the jewels in his other. They were no longer glowing. "The magic is gone, Baron Castellan."

"But...the dragon..."

"The dragon is not a danger, but that amulet was." She stepped forward, holding out her hand. The baron dropped the gems and chain into her open palm.

They were now harmless obsidian and opal, the silver setting dented and empty.

Alex held them in her hand and looked to Orion. The Royal Guards were forcing Baron Salomon's soldiers to unlock to chains and remove them from Orion, per her command. Orion stood still, watching the soldiers do their work, smoke curling upward from his nostrils.

Baron Rothschilde walked down the steps. "Your majesty, are you certain there is no danger from the dragon?"

"Positive."

The soldiers fumbled with the locks and it seemed to take much longer to release them than it had taken to fasten them. Orion huffed and a plume of thick smoke rose skyward.

Alex met his turquoise gaze and nodded.

The dragon turned its head to the sky, then brought it back down to look at her.

"Move away from the dragon." Though Alex did not yell, her voice remained strong and carried to all who listened. Most of the court had moved back when the soldiers had moved to free Orion, and they had been quiet, watching and waiting.

The Royal Guard immediately obeyed, pulling Baron Salomon's men back with them.

Orion shook his head and began the transformation back to human.

Alex watched, smiling. She glanced to Sir Oliver, and found him not watching Orion, but the guards.

Grinning at him, she winked. "I will not let anyone harm him."

"I know." But Sir Oliver did not stop watching the others, his hands grasping the scabbard where his sword should have been.

Lady Chantelle was also searching the crowd, but she appeared to be looking for someone in particular.

"Lady Chantelle?" Alex noted that Orion was fully human again and that everyone stared at him.

"I thought my father might be here, seeking assistance in rescuing me."

"We will summon him. Do not worry." Alex turned back to Orion. "Welcome back. It is good to see your face again."

"It is good to have my face again. I was beginning to think I would be as before." Orion strode forward, but the Royal Guard stopped him.

Alex shook her head and pushed them away, winding her arms around Orion, ignoring the gasps around her. "I was worried for you."

"I was worried for you. Since they did not know who you truly were, I thought they might harm you." Orion's arms twined around her, squeezing. He dropped a quick kiss on the top of her head, and the caress made her insides quiver.

Alex stepped back and Orion's arms fell away. "I am well and we are back."

Lady Chantelle gasped. "Papa!" The young woman lifted her skirts in a most unladylike fashion and sprinted across the courtyard toward an elderly gentleman in a green velvet tunic and brown trousers.

"Ah. Perhaps I won't have to summon Lord Sousong to the castle."

Watching the reunion, how the two held each other and whispered, only to hug each other again, Alex thought of her own parents. King Edric and Queen Alina were still caught in the tapestry.

What if the amulet could have freed them? The stones in her hand warmed then heated enough to burn.

She dropped them to the ground, examining the pinkening of her skin, running a finger over the developing blister.

"What happened?" Orion took her hand, running his own fingers over the wound.

"They started to burn when I thought of the tapestry and my parents."

"Burn?"

Alex nodded. She wasn't sure if that meant they could have freed them or not.

Orion stooped to examine the stones, touching one with a single finger. "They are very similar to the ones your uncle used on me."

"Be careful." She grabbed his shoulder to stop him from picking them up. "We don't know what they might do."

"What is going on?" Baron Humphrey loomed over them.

Straightening, Alex stared at the baron. "Weren't you paying attention?"

Baron Castellan, still on the steps, snickered; Baron Rothschilde turned to hide his own smile.

"You are visiting your grandparents." The young baron spoke like his words would make it true.

"I'm afraid not. That was simply a ruse so I could leave for an extended period without you giving me trouble."

Baron Humphrey pointed a solid finger in her face. "Giving you trouble? I'll have you-"

The baron's words were cut off when Orion stood, pushed the finger away, and stepped in front of Alex. "I'd mind my words if I were you. And that finger."

"You're not me, are you?" Baron Humphrey had to look up to stare Orion in the face.

"Good thing." Alex piped up. "And he's giving you very good advice, Baron. You might consider heeding it."

"I have never-"

"Nor will you ever." This time, it was Alex who did not let him finish. "I do believe I can function with only two advisors. Please consider this your notice."

Baron Humphrey stood in the middle of the court, his mouth opening and closing like that of an ornamental koi in a pond. Red-suited soldiers scurried around him, smiling, some even chuckling.

Alex addressed her two remaining advisors. "Baron Castellan, please see to the prisoners. I would like Baron Salomon in solitary confinement in the dungeons. His soldiers can be incarcerated in the usual manner. Baron Rothschilde, please see that refreshments are made available for my friends. It has been a long day or two, and I think they are in need of some pampering."

"Yes, of course, Your Highness." Baron Castellan clicked his heels and nodded to the soldiers holding the former Baron

Salomon. The man was dragged back toward the entry to the dungeon stairs.

"You can't do this to me! I'm a baron for god's sake!"

One of the guards placed a hand over the baron's mouth, stifling his cries. "She said you aren't."

"I will see to refreshments immediately, Your Majesty. In the Great Hall?"

"Nay. The library, please."

Baron Rothschilde bowed and marched back to the castle, motioning for the curious maids, who had ventured out to see the commotion, to reenter the castle and make preparations.

Baron Humphrey sneered. "And what of Baron Salomon's holding?"

"Sir Oliver?" Alex turned to her new friend.

"Yes, Alex? Beg your pardon, I mean, yes, Princess Alexandrina?" A tide of color rose in the young man's cheeks at his faux pas, though his bow was still as elegant as ever.

"Are you leaving Vreden soon?"

"I was hoping to stay for a while. There is not much waiting for me in Paixor." His gaze drifted to Lady Chantelle, who stood secure in her father's embrace.

"Very good. I will ask that you oversee the holding in question while I consider its ultimate fate. I should think it would take only a couple of months for the rest of my barons to make a case to me for their management of those lands."

Sir Oliver straightened, his eyes wide. "You want me to watch over an entire holding?" His surprise made him forget to correct his familiarity.

"Indeed." Alex winked and nodded her head to the far end of the courtyard. "I am sure Lord Sousong will be happy to have an ally as his neighbor for the immediate future."

The young man glanced to Lady Chantelle again, a smile of delight spreading across his cheeks. "Of course, Your Majesty. I would be my honor to watch over that holding for you in the interim."

"Your highness?" Baron Rothschilde stood once again on the steps. "All is waiting for you and your guests in the library."

Sighing, Alex nodded and started up the steps. "Thank you, Baron. Please relay my offer of refreshment to Lord Sousong and his daughter." She gestured in Lady Chantelle's direction. Though, Sir Oliver might make the invitation before Baron Rothschilde got the chance. The young man was striding toward the young lady, head up and hand outstretched to greet her father.

"Of course." Baron Rothschilde clicked his heels and bowed.

Orion followed Alex up the steps to the castle. The courtyard was nearly empty now, save for the wagon and the soldiers guarding the gate--and a few noisy children chasing chickens it the far corner and Baron Humphrey who seemed rooted to his spot on the cobbles. "So, Princess, what will you do now?"

Alex turned at the top step, the added height allowing her to look directly into Orion's steady gaze. She smiled. "Learn to rule, but by doing it, rather than watching others do it. It is time I carved my own path, I think."

"Carved? Path?" Orion took another step, so that he had to look down at her just a bit. That step took him close enough that Alex could feel his heated breath upon her cheek.

"Yes. Toward the future I want."

"And what do you want in your future? I wonder if it anything like what I want in mine?" Orion bent his head towards hers, his lids at half-mast.

Stifling a giggle, Alex shoved her friend and raced into the castle. "Let's go ask Old Bertram."

"You don't need to go ask anyone!" Orion chased after her. "Ally, get back here!"

But Alex skidded on the foyer tiles, using a marble post to catch her momentum and spin herself around to hide. She lurked just inside the castle door, waiting.

When Orion jogged past, she pounced, laughing hard at his jump at the attack.

"What?" The startled young man grabbed at her waist.

Alex smiled up at Orion and licked her lips, raising her hands to his broad shoulders. Raising on tip toe, she whispered. "This is what I see in my future."

And she kissed him.

CHAPTER THIRTY-FIVE

The yelling broke them apart, Ally with a gasp and Orion with a groan.

"What is it?" Ally pushed away, jogging to the still open doors.

Orion followed, stopping just behind her to look out over her head.

The female dragon circled overhead, dipping down close to the wagon, only to soar up again when the red-clad guards roared back at her.

"Stop." Ally trotted out, waving her hands at her guards.

"Princess! Get back inside." The head guard ran to her, trying to block her from reaching the stairs to descend to the melee.

"No, it's fine." Ally glanced over her shoulder, "Can you still communicate with her Orion?"

"Not like this. Give me a minute."

"Why so long?" Ally frowned.

"Right now, after..." Orion flipped his hands around at her, "I'm cemented in my human form. I need to find the dragon again."

Smirking, ally watched him close his eyes, pressing the lids together while he concentrated.

"Don't let them hurt her." Lady Chantelle ran to Ally. "She just wants her egg."

"I know." Ally reached out for her friend's hand, squeezing it tight. "It's all right. Her egg is in the wagon. Back away and let her land."

The guards walked back from the wagon, swords out, arms wide to keep the villagers behind them. They left the wagon in a wide empty circle.

Landing in a swoop of wings and dust, the female dragon stretched its neck up and out, belching a dingle flame of fire skyward.

"Orion, talk to her."

The heavy sigh from beside her was fully human. "I can't. The dragon is gone for the moment. Sorry." Orion's teal eyes darkened.

"S'okay. Maybe she'll understand we don't want to hurt her or her egg." Ally didn't go down the steps though, and pulled Chantelle behind her a bit.

Oliver joined them, along with Chantelle's father.

"Is the egg still in the chest?" Oliver whispered, ducking down to make sure everyone heard.

"Yes." Ally groaned. Why hadn't she thought about releasing the egg? She'd been so focused on her small victory and Orion, she'd not even considered the plight of the female dragon and her baby.

"Is there any way to make her understand it's in there?" Oliver's voice rose.

Taking a deep breath, Ally stepped forward. "Everyone stay back."

"Ally." Orion's hiss felt like a solid push. "Let me."

"But-"

"I have the dragon inside, perhaps she will sense it and listen. Or at least, not shred me with her claws."

"I do not find that overly comforting."

Lady Chantelle grabbed Ally's arm. "Perhaps, if we show her the broken amulet?"

Ally blinked at her friend and nodded. "Good idea. Perhaps I need a third advisor after all. Let me know if you are interested in the position."

Orion pulled the gems and empty chain from his pocket, lying them out on the step in front of him.

The female dragon shifted forward, sniffing the air, here gaze never leaving the sparkling gems.

"The egg is in the wagon." Orion pointed at the wagon, which now shook and a rumbling could be heard from inside.

"I'm not sure it's still an egg." Ally stared at Orion. "We need to get it out of that chest."

The female dragon cocked its head to the side, watching Ally.

Ally pointed at the wagon. "Let me help?"

The dragon stepped back and Ally took it as a sign that she could approach the wagon. She glanced at Orion beside her. "Come with me?"

Orion nodded and took the first step, eyeing the great beast before them.

The dragon did not move, and so he continued down, one step at a time.

Ally followed, just as slow, one hand resting on his shoulder. When they reached the wagon, she peeked inside.

The chest was no longer in the center, two of its chains broken so that it was on its side, but still latched tight.

"Poor, baby. Bet you're terrified."

The mama dragon whined.

"Whatever you're going to do Ally, hurry." Orion stood watch at the back. "I think mama understands that her baby is trapped."

Ally swallowed hard and pulled on the cold, letting its icy tendrils reach into her fingers, crawling into the back of the wagon, she stared at the first metal clasp and reach out a finger to touch it.

Ice formed on the clasp, winding into the mechanism, expanding until the metal cracked and burst.

One down.

She touched the second clasp, breaking it as well.

Once done, she jumped back, expecting the lid to drop down and a baby dragon to fly out.

But it didn't.

"Ally?"

"I'm working on it." She pushed the cold back down, but it was hard. Her magic hadn't hurt the egg, had it?

She pulled the lid down and the egg rolled out, a large crack down one side, oozing a slimy pink goo.

"Orion? Do you know what it looks like when an egg hatches?"

"Not really. Brood females were kept separate from the males." His voice cracked. "Um, Ally?"

Looking over her shoulder, Ally found herself up close and personal with the female dragon.

The dragon nudged the egg and it rolled again, leaving a trail of the goo behind. Snorting, the dragon washed the egg with her hot breath, and it jerked and rolled all on its own.

Mama nuzzled the egg, snorting more hot air over it so that it rocked and the crack widened.

In a burst of shell and pink slime, the egg exploded, fragments of shell sticking all over Ally, pasted to her with the goo.

"Ugh!"

"Ally?" Orion pushed the mam dragon's wing aside to look in.

"We're good." Ally pulled a large triangle of shell out of her hair, the goop stringing like melted cheese. "Look it."

The little dragon, shimmering pink and peach scales covered in matching slime, whined and wobbled on spindly legs.

Mama dragon cooed and the baby tottered toward the sound.

"Oh, thank goodness." Ally relaxed into the mess and smiled.

Orion grinned back; the mama dragon didn't seem to mind him tucked beneath her wing. "He doesn't look like he'll be flying any time soon."

"No."

The baby's wings were limp and wet and plastered to its little body. The female blew a soft waft of warm air over it, and the soft natal scales quivered.

"I guess we'll have a couple of extra visitors to the castle for a few days." Ally sighed, watching the pair. "It's the least we can do."

"Least?" Orion snorted. "Ally, you saved the baby's life."

"Oh, I'm pretty sure mama would have come to the rescue." Ally reached out tentative fingers and scratched behind the big dragon's ear.

The female canted her head, so Ally had better access.

"So, the Dragon Queen of Vreden." Orion leaned against the wagon's vertical frame.

"No. Queen Ally of Vreden, Friend to Dragons. That's what I'll be called."

Orion shook his head, a slight grin softening his features. "We'll see what gets written in the history books."

To be continued...

T. L. Frye